A TRACE OF COPPER

An Elemental Web Tale — A Novella

Anne Renwick

Enjoy!
Anne Renwick

www.annerenwick.com

Book Layout ©2015 BookDesignTemplates.com

A Trace of Copper/ Anne Renwick. -- 1st ed.
ISBN 978-0-9977475-5-3

Cover design by James T. Egan of Bookfly Design.

Edited by Sandra Sookoo.

To every woman who ever worked in the biological sciences and medical fields

THANK YOU TO...

Rajendrani Mukopadhyay. You helped bring my heroine to life and corrected me again and again. Any remaining missteps are my own. Sorry about the corset (not really).

Huw Erith, Aled Edwards and Ynyr Roberts for saving my Welsh. The internet proved a poor subsitute for native speakers.

The Plotmonkeys: Shaunee Cole, Kristan Higgins, Jennifer Iszkiewicz and Huntley Fitzpatrick. The inspiration for this novella took root and began to grow during one of our precious weekends. Your friendship means everything.

Sandra Sookoo, my wonderful editor who mercilessly ferrets out weaknesses and sets my work on a better course.

My husband and my two boys who are still laughing over the opening line.
My mom and dad who instilled in me a love of both reading and travel.
Mr. Fox and his red pen.

CHAPTER ONE

Aberwyn, Wales
Spring, 1885

"It bit me," the young woman informed Piyali, hiking her skirts and rolling down her woolen hose. "Right through my stocking." Miss Price, the shopkeeper's daughter, plopped down on a chair and propped her foot upon a stool, pointing. "And now it's blue."

Dr. Piyali Mukherji leaned closer. As insane as Miss Price's words sounded, they rang true. Her ankle was indeed blue.

Well, part of it. There was a decided lesion approximately two inches in diameter above her fibular protuberance. Piyali pressed two fingers against the blemish. She would describe it as an infection. Except it didn't appear inflamed, and it wasn't hot to the touch.

And it was *blue*.

Unheard of. But that was why she'd accepted the Crown's commission, taken on the added duties of a Queen's agent. The Duke of Avesbury, the gentleman at the head of this small, select group, had offered her a chance to be on the forefront of investigations into strange and unusual medical conditions. This certainly fit the bill.

"A frog bit you." Piyali's eyebrows rose, hoping she'd heard wrong. "A blue frog. With teeth." Did frogs have teeth? And frogs—at least in Britain—were supposed to be green. Or brown.

Miss Price bit her lip. It didn't bode well that she needed to consider her story.

Hoping for an explanation, she looked to the man who loomed beside her taking up far too much space in the small parlor. Time had turned familiar into foreign. Mr. Evan Tredegar wore his dark, tousled curls longer, no cravat wound under his collar beneath the rough shadow of his beard, and a small, curved scar cut through the edge of his right eyebrow. Under her study, a muscle twitched at his jawline, and his lips pressed into a thin line. He refused to meet her gaze. Perhaps it was just as well, for his eyes never failed to ignite a slow burn beneath her skin, and she needed to focus.

Still, a certain unease gave her pause. Once she'd been able to read his every mood and would have labeled his expression as concerned. Except the man she'd known wouldn't withhold information vital to a patient's treatment. What wasn't he telling her?

"Miss Price?" Piyali prompted.

The young woman nodded. "Then it hopped away and disappeared into the woods." Sticking her lower lip out in a pout, she looked up at her mother. "Is this really necessary? Besides, she can't be a real doctor. How can a *woman* hold such a degree?" With a sidelong glance at Piyali's clothing, her voice dropped to a whisper. "An *Indian* woman."

A real doctor. Piyali resisted the urge to roll her eyes. If she had a shilling for every time she'd heard that sentiment... Instead, she lifted her chin and replied, "I attended medical school at the Université de Paris where women have been accepted since 1860."

Never had Paris seemed so far away. Four of the best—and worst—years of her life. She'd earned her place there by being twice as good as the other students, most of them men. Any who had sneered at her inclusion swiftly adjusted their opinion as she collected one award after another, graduating first in her class. As to the prejudice, she no longer felt the need to justify the traditional clothing she wore. If a person could not appreciate the richness and intricacy of Indian designs, then it was their loss.

With an unsteady hand, Mrs. Price patted her daughter on the shoulder and threw Piyali a nervous look. "Lister University's choice of medical practitioner is alarming. No doubt Dr. Mukherji was all they could spare, but I have every confidence in Mr. Tredegar's ointment. The blue stain has barely spread since you first applied it. In fact, I think it's grown smaller." From the pinched expression on her face, the woman clearly wished Piyali elsewhere. "But your father worries and wanted to consult a board-certified physician in case amputation becomes necessary."

"Amputation!" Miss Price's chest began to heave, her eyes growing wide, her fingers digging into the cushion of her chair. "It's just a spot!"

"A very unusual spot." Evan finally spoke, though his words were tight and strained. "One that must be examined by someone with more expertise than myself."

Resentment sparked. His defense of her skills was unwelcome. Both by her and, judging from the deep frown upon her face, Miss Price.

Piyali glanced again at the blue lesion. Could it be no more than a stain of blue ink? Had she interrupted a hoax, a bizarre courtship trick designed to lure a handsome, young pharmacist into this parlor? For upon her arrival, her purported patient had been fluttering eyelashes and casting Evan glances drenched with unfulfilled longing. Or—she narrowed her eyes—did the fault lie squarely on Evan's shoulders? Did he toy with the young shopkeeper's daughter, making promises he couldn't—or wouldn't—keep?

For once he'd made her promises, ones she'd clung to for four long years abroad. Promises he'd failed to keep when he returned from his overseas voyage some three months ago. Upholding her own vow, she'd sent him a message, then pounced upon the daily post for days—weeks—hoping for word of his imminent arrival, but... nothing. Save a devastating silence.

Heartache must have shown upon her face, for her mother had hunted down coconuts and banana leaves before taking herself down into the kitchens of their London townhouse to personally oversee the preparation of Piyali's favorite dish, *bhetki macher paturi*—marinated steamed fish—in an effort to coax her to eat something... anything. Food wasn't her mother's only crisis response. Gentlemen of all kinds had begun to appear around the dining table. At first they were Bengali, then merely Indian. She knew her mother grew desperate when a six-foot-four, blond Swede had joined them.

"Choose a husband, Piyali," Ma had begged, reminding her that if her father were still alive, he would even now be arranging her marriage. Even Piyali's British stepfather conspired to assist Ma, making noises about grandchildren. But no other man, no matter how accomplished or handsome, could mend the rift in her life.

An acidic pain had lodged itself beneath her heart, slowly corroding all of her hopes and dreams. Though she'd buried herself in her work, establishing a research program in her laboratory while training to become a Queen's agent, nothing eased the ache.

Which was why she'd cringed when Mr. Black, the duke's right-hand spy, had handed her this first assignment. "Aberwyn, Wales?" she'd read. Evan lived there.

"Two birds, one stone." The agent's eyes had sparkled with mischief. "A competent research pharmacist and a specialist in infectious disease reconnecting over a mysterious and peculiar illness." He'd laughed. "What could go wrong?"

Though she'd wanted to cry, orders were orders. She'd packed a trunk with the essentials and boarded the first train to Cardiff, enduring lewd stares and bawdy speculations about the bedroom predilections of *exotic* young women. Aether, how she hated that word. In Cardiff, she bought a ticket for a rickety steamstage, one that had broken down twice en route to Aberwyn. There, despite her exhortations to be careful, the driver had tossed her trunk from the roof onto the muddy street where a grumbling stable boy had dragged it—bumping up each step—to a small, cramped room above the town's only tavern, *Yr Ysgyfarnog Wen*—The White Hare. Later, a short walk along the rutted main street had brought her here, to the shopkeeper's cottage.

"Are you all right?" Evan's voice was soft and considerate.

"Merely contemplating treatment options," she lied.

The long hours spent traveling had jarred every joint and coated her with a film of dust, all while doubts gnawed at her mind. But deceitful hopes kept whispering that perhaps Evan's missive had gone astray and so, though exhausted, she'd taken special pains for their first meeting in five years.

Shaking the travel wrinkles free, she'd donned a favorite green lehenga—skirt—with a simple, paisley embroidered border edging the hem. Buckling her corset atop the matching half-sleeved choli, she'd brushed her long, wavy hair to a shine before twisting a green, satin ribbon into a plait over her shoulder. But his eyes hadn't flashed with desire, his pulse hadn't jumped in his throat, and his fingers hadn't twitched—as they once had—with a need to touch her skin. Evan had barely looked at her at all.

The ache settled back into her chest. It was no use, clinging to the past. She kept her gaze fixed upon her patient, trying to anesthetize her response, for it hurt too much to gaze upon Evan's once familiar face, to fight the urge to smooth his unkempt curls and drag her palm over the roughness of his cheeks.

"Ointment?" she asked, pulling a decilamp from its loop upon her leather corset, shaking it to activate the bioluminescent bacteria within. She bent over Miss Price's foot, directing a beam of light at the lesion. There. At its center, a tiny, curved, pink line. A scratch—bite? —that had already healed. Possibly the entry point of whatever organism had invaded her skin.

"An ointment of *khu-neh-ari*," Evan replied, speaking a foreign word that likely originated deep within the Amazonian rainforest, "made from the *Caniramon divaritum*, a climbing shrub."

She glanced at him out of the corner of her eye. "Have you encountered this particular ailment before?"

"I've been unable to identify it." He shifted on his feet. "Though the outward progression of its margins is reminiscent of a fungal infection. Hence the ointment."

"Infection!" The older woman yanked her hand from her daughter's shoulder.

"Fungus!" In a move worthy of Drury Lane, Miss Price threw herself backward upon the chair and tossed an arm across her forehead.

"Possible, but—" Piyali shifted the beam of light and the lesion... sparkled? She flicked the light away, then back. For a second, the skin shimmered, flashing pink and silver. Then, once again, it was blue. Not good. "I'm going to need a biopsy."

"Biopsy?" Miss Price's voice quivered, and she squirmed on her seat. "What's that?"

Turning to her bag of medical equipment, Piyali extracted a glass aetheroscope slide, a few eyedropper bottles of stain and a sterile razor, arranging them all upon the small side table. "I'm going to shave away a tiny portion of the surface of your skin so that I might analyze it beneath my aetheroscope. You should feel no more than a slight pinch."

Miss Price whimpered.

With a long-suffering sigh, Evan reached out to take Miss Price's hand. Odd that he wore gloves inside the parlor. "Squeeze as tight as you feel you must."

Minutes later, the skin sample was prepped and loaded within her small, portable aetheroscope. Once the light source was activated, Piyali screwed in a pressurized canister of aether, listening to the gas hiss as it filled the chamber of the device. Perched on the edge of a chair, she bent over, peering through the eyepiece to adjust focus and magnification.

"Interesting," she murmured under her breath, then changed the angle of illumination. The color shifted.

A brush of feet on carpet. The faint disturbance of the air around her as Evan crossed the room to her side and leaned close. "What is it?" The heat of his breath swept across the bare skin of her neck and sent uninvited shivers across her skin.

How was it one man could affect her so?

She took a deep, steadying breath before answering. "A pearly luster." Still, her voice caught. He was much too close. "One that tends toward iridescence of the pink and blue variety. It could be..." She dialed in to the highest resolution and stifled a curse. As feared, the jolting of the steamstage—or the tossing of her trunk— had indeed broken valuable equipment. Shaking her head, she stood and stepped back from the aetheroscope—and away from Evan. "My objective, the one with the highest resolution? Its crystalline lens is cracked."

She could guess, but she wouldn't. Not even for Evan. Especially not for him. He knew something, and he wasn't sharing. Childish of her, but now that she too knew something, she wasn't sharing either. Resolve stiffened her spine. He could wait—they all could—until she confirmed her findings with cold, hard evidence.

"Piyali?" Evan prompted.

Mother and daughter drew offended breaths at his overly informal address of an unfamiliar and unmarried woman. Even in a small Welsh village, propriety must be maintained.

"Dr. Mukherji," she corrected him, her voice cool and clinical. Unless Evan decided to share whatever he concealed, there was nothing more she could do today. She was tired and hungry and irritated. And a report was due to Mr. Black. "I can't say for certain. Further tests are required."

A light mist of rain dampened Evan's hair as he stood in the street staring at the door of *Yr Ysgyfarnog Wen*. If only he could turn back time.

Five years and she was still as beautiful as ever. He had no right to look, no right to steal glances. But he had. Of dark eyes he'd once stared into. Of long, wavy hair he'd once twined about his fingers. Of deep pink lips he'd once kissed.

He'd done his best not to stare, not to notice how the graceful arc of her collarbone peeked from beneath the edge of her neckline, how a short corset clasped her narrow waist beneath its tooled, leather surface, how her skirt flared outward over generous hips, or how its raised hemline revealed ankles encased in laced boots.

Her corset was studded with metal loops, hooks and chains to which she'd clipped all manner of essential devices and tools. Including a government-issued TTX pistol that gave his pulse a jolt. Was there anything more alluring than a strong, competent woman? But it was the familiar, amber glass vial dangling from a chain beside her hip that focused his gaze. Wondering, he'd bent close to peer through the aetheroscope and inhaled. Essence of orange blossoms. All these years she'd kept it, the same essential oil still scenting the water that rinsed her hair. Long-suppressed desires stirred.

He closed his eyes. He had no right to such thoughts.

Not one week after he'd returned to Britain's shores, a skeet pigeon with rust-tipped wings had alighted upon his window sill, a brief note tied to its jointed ankle with news of her degree and the direction to her family's London townhouse. To speed his reply, she'd even included a punched return card for the clockwork bird.

With stars in his eyes, he'd sat down in his tropical greenhouse to put pen to paper. Halfway through his letter a small, blue frog had leapt onto the back of his hand. A stowaway upon one of the many lianas— climbing vines—he'd brought back from his voyage to the Amazonian rainforest. He'd thought the shimmering creature cute, adorable, delightful.

Until it bit him.

Evan rubbed his thumb and forefinger together, the soft black leather of his gloves reminding him of the moment everything went wrong. He'd never sent that letter. Or any letter. One didn't ask the woman he loved to share a slow descent into madness.

Time passed, and the vine of his silence slowly twined itself about his throat, growing so thick that only a machete could cut it free. Too late to ask her for help now. Not only did she likely despise him, she was a Queen's agent.

Nonetheless, he must speak with her. Her aetheroscope was broken and that meant she would want to return to London on the morning's steamstage. That couldn't happen. He couldn't allow her to leave, not with a sample of Miss Price's skin in her possession. Here, in Wales, things could be kept under control.

Stopping her meant entering The White Hare where one Miss Sarah Parker, the tavern's daughter, would be lying in wait. He willed his feet to move, to cross the rutted road, willed his hand to wrap around the iron handle of the tavern's door and pull it open.

"Evan!" Sarah cried, her voice a confection of icing and spun sugar. Wiping her hands on her apron, she rushed to his side.

Out of the proverbial pan and into the fire.

Three months ago, Sarah and Miss Price—Tegan, she insisted whenever her mother wasn't around—had begun fighting to gain his attention, all in a futile effort to secure a marriage proposal. Their bickering was a constant reminder of what he would never have, a thorn that pricked at his conscience.

Tegan found any remotely credible excuse to throw herself in his path. Unchaperoned, she regularly dropped by his cottage—a three-mile walk into the countryside—to request more packets of headache powder and throat lozenges for the shop. Chances she sold that much were close to zero.

And Sarah? She pounced on him every time he stepped into The White Hare, always ready with a pint of his favorite ale, begging for tales of his time in the rainforest even as she tugged the bodice of her dress scandalously low. Worse, her parents aided and abetted, turning a blind eye to her blatant flirtations and not calling her to task when she ignored the other customers.

"Miss Parker," he replied. "Where is Dr. Mukherji? I need to speak with her."

Wrapping her arm about his, Sarah urged him closer to the peat fire burning in the grate. "Upstairs," she admitted, playfully pushing him into a chair and dropping into his lap. "But I'm right here."

"Sarah," he warned in a low voice. "I've asked you not to—"

She leaned forward, pressing generous breasts against his chest while twisting a finger into his curls so tightly it threatened to rip his hair from its roots. "Oh, *please*. All these months you've been without a woman to warm your bed. You need a wife, one who can help you run that pharmacy of yours in Cardiff. Tegan might know business, but she's far too uptight to keep you satisfied after hours."

"Stop," he snapped, grabbing her hips and shoving her away. "I've no intention of taking a wife."

Laughing, Sarah caught her balance on the sticky tabletop. "No? Then you'd best be careful. The Indian princess can't take her eyes off you." The lift of her chin redirected his attention.

What? He whipped his head about, catching Piyali's narrow-eyed gaze from across the room as she descended the stairs. Guilt stuck in his throat. He'd not been unfaithful and didn't want her to think... Did it matter? Her eyes slid away, and she turned her back, climbing onto a stool at the bar. A deliberate move to avoid any and all private conversation.

"She's not a princess," he said.

"Oh?" Her voice rose in a teasing lilt. "Then why do you stare at her as if she wears a crown of gold and precious jewels?"

Evan glowered. "Please, just bring me a pint."

"Of course," Sarah said, then winked. "And I'll see what I can do about a little something extra." She sauntered away, swinging her hips with each step. Tossing a quick word to her father, she jerked her head in Evan's direction. Then, sliding onto a stool, Sarah turned her bright eyes upon Piyali. Her lips moved, and Piyali laughed. Not good. Sarah's interference was akin to swatting a bee hive with a stick. The dull, throbbing beginnings of a splitting headache began to hammer away at his skull.

Glass banged on wood as Mr. Parker dropped a pint of frothy ale onto the table before him. "The way you've been handling my daughter? I think we ought to speak about calling banns."

Evan dropped his head into his hands.

CHAPTER TWO

"So tell me, is the all-too-precious Miss Tegan Price going to live?" The blonde, blue-eyed serving girl dropped onto a stool beside Piyali and leaned close. "Not that I wish her ill," she hastened to add, "just that we've been at each other's throats fighting over Evan." She waved a dismissive hand in the air. "Tegan's always fabricating one ailment or another, any excuse for Evan to formulate her a new potion." Her voice dropped to a whisper. "Not only is he the most handsome man for miles around, he has a shop in Cardiff, and both of us want out of this dismal village." A deep sigh slid from her lips. "Not that he wants anything to do with either of us."

Piyali blinked at the sudden onslaught of unsolicited information. "I'm sorry, I can't discuss a patient's health," she said. Then, reminding herself she was an agent tasked with collecting information, forced herself to sip the bitter ale and plaster on a conspiratorial smile. "But please, feel free to share any and all gossip about her with me."

A wide grin split the woman's face. "We're going to be great friends," she announced, slapping a hand upon the bar top. "I'm Sarah Parker, daughter of this humble establishment. Sorry about the shameful display of overt flirting you had to witness. What *is* your trick? Evan can't seem to take his eyes off you."

"It's not what you think," she began, but a discordant note rang in her answer. "We knew each other once, long ago."

"And now find yourselves forced to work together to cure Tegan of whatever it is that ails her." Sarah held up a hand. "Which you can't talk about, but it's good to know you're not added competition." She leaned forward, eyes wide, waiting. "So tell me instead, are you from India?" She continued before Piyali could draw breath. "I love the embroidery on your skirt. I've always wanted to travel, but the only other place I've ever been—not counting Cardiff—is London." She sighed. "I miss London."

Sensing an easily won ally, Piyali shared a bit more than she would otherwise. "I was born in northeast India, but moved here as a young girl with my stepfather and mother. Aside from the four years I studied in Paris, I've lived in London." After an epidemic of diphtheria tore her family to shreds, her mother had resisted remarrying, choosing to support them by selling the stunning *kantha* shawls she hand stitched, until a chance encounter with a British textile importer had brought her stepfather into their lives. Ignoring the many yelling and pleading aunties and uncles, they'd married and moved to England. Her mother had found a second chance at love... could she?

"Paris!" Sarah's eyes grew hazy. "I'm so jealous. It's awful here, but my father lost his job over a bar fight and decided he'd open his own tavern. Here. In Wales." She rolled her eyes. "I've no idea why. It's so remote. And forget about learning Welsh! It's impossible to wrap the tongue about. Just try to say the name of this tavern."

Piyali made her best attempt, and they both dissolved into tears of laughter.

"See?" Sarah said, then lowered her voice to a whisper as she waggled her eyebrows. "Thing is, I understand it just fine. Makes it fun to listen in on all the gossip."

"Sarah!" Mr. Parker yelled, beckoning his daughter. "Enough. Back to work."

Feeling as if she'd struck gold, Piyali pressed a hand atop Sarah's. "You'll tell me more about this town later?" Perhaps it was a path to nothing but renewed pain, but she needed to know about Evan, about what he'd been up to since his return.

"Only if you tell me more about India. And Paris."

"Agreed."

Sarah hopped onto her feet and turned back to the customers.

Sensing Evan's stare between her shoulder blades, Piyali took a deep breath and turned. Sad blue eyes met hers. Why hadn't he answered her message? Perhaps he'd fallen in love with another? Her chest constricted. They *had* been apart far longer than they'd been together.

Her heart had almost healed. Almost. Not that she would be giving him a chance to tear another hole by squabbling with Sarah and Tegan. It didn't matter what kept him silent. He'd made his choice.

His eyebrows drew together. Good. He ought to feel guilty about never answering her message. If he'd changed his mind, it was simple decency to inform her that she no longer fit into his life plans.

Difficult as it was, she needed to speak with him. She needed to know what he knew about the blue lesion and, to meet the bare minimum requirement of her mission, she needed to deliver Mr. Black's invitation.

She spun on her seat to face the bar and waved Mr. Parker over.

"Hungry?" he asked.

"No." She placed a punch card, a rolled parchment in a tin canister and two coins upon the bar. "Rather, I'd like to charter your skeet pigeon." The clockwork bird didn't look particularly airworthy. She frowned. "If it's in working order."

"Tends to malfunction," he warned, his voice suggesting she wasted perfectly good money. "Even on a good day, doesn't make it much past London."

Worth a try. It was the only bird in town, and she hadn't seen any telegraph wires. If Mr. Black couldn't arrange to have a new crystalline lens objective shipped, she'd take her sample back for analysis in her laboratory at Lister University. Waiting a few days for an answer would give her time to keep an eye on Tegan's lesion. "Good enough."

He pocketed the coins and, as he turned to tie the tin canister to the bird's ankle, his wife burst through the door, a bloody rag wrapped about her finger. Glaring at her husband, she pushed past him and plunged her hand into a bucket of soapy water all the while muttering under her breath about stupid plans and unreasonable men.

"What happened?" Sarah asked, handing her mother a clean cloth.

"It's nothing." Mrs. Parker dried her hands. "I scratched myself on some thorns by Seren's Well."

"The fairy well?" Sarah hissed. "You didn't. Tell me you didn't."

The steam in her mother's answering stare could make the nearby copper teakettle whistle. "I did it for you," she snapped.

"You can't," Sarah spat back. "That's the whole point. Do you know what the other girls will say if they find out?" She stalked away.

As Sarah's mother struggled to bandage her finger, Piyali offered, "I'm a doctor. I can look at it if you'd like."

Mrs. Parker's head jerked up. For a long moment, she stared at Piyali, her face expressionless. "More than a doctor, I'd say. Everyone knows what the Price Family is up to, pulling strings to drag you all the way here from London." Her mouth twisted. "Bet they were mightily disappointed when a woman arrived. And a foreigner at that. Nothing they'd like better than to see their precious daughter wed to a man of influence."

Piyali sucked in a sharp breath of air. She *was* a citizen, granted as a royal prerogative when she joined the Queen's agents, an offer only extended by special invitation. By working as a British spy, she had done— and would do—far, far more to serve this country than most natural born citizens. All this, however, was not something one announced, particularly in a Welsh tavern.

"Elena," her husband growled in warning, "there's no need to air the dirty laundry of others."

"*Hmphff.*" Mrs. Parker snatched a rag and set to wiping the far end of the counter.

A hand touched her shoulder, and Piyali jumped.

"It's me." Evan's voice was hushed. "We need to speak. The rain has stopped. Perhaps a walk?"

Given the hostile glances the tavern owners hurled at each other like poison-tipped darts, Piyali was all too happy to flee. "I'll grab my overcoat."

"What's this about a fairy well?" Piyali asked him.

Lines of irritation pulled at the corners of her mouth. Insulted by the Parkers, most likely. They were experts at open hostility and masters of harsh insults. How they'd managed to conceive a daughter, he'd never know.

"*Ffynnon Seren.* Seren's Well. A bit of local tradition and legend," he answered, happy to let more serious topics wait until the dark cloud lifted from her face. "A pretty little spot just outside the village. Come, I'll show you."

Evan didn't offer her his arm. He wasn't a gentleman, and she wasn't a lady. Besides, it was better if they didn't touch. He wouldn't want to let go.

Despite all they had to say to each other, they walked in silence beneath the gray sky, following a narrow, winding path into a wooded gully. As they neared the well, he waved her ahead of him, not wanting to obscure her view of the ancient holy site. A small pool edged by rocks collected the upwelling of water beneath an old tree. Its roots had twisted and turned, invading the crevices of the ruins that stood beside the well. Overhead, scraps of cloth tied to its branches fluttered in the wind. Rough stepping stones led downward to the cool, clear water.

"It's beautiful. And so very peaceful. Like a *pabitro pukur*..." She trailed her fingers over the moss-covered stones of a low wall. "What was this?"

"An alter? A shrine? A chapel?" He shrugged. "No one recalls. But," he couldn't suppress a smile at the ridiculous legend he was about to share, "tradition has it that one can cure epilepsy by bathing in the pool at midnight while holding a duck beneath one's left arm."

"A duck?" Her face lit up as she laughed. "Are there any other odd traditions?"

"Too many to count. All invocations involve an offering of a bent steel pin to the water-sprite who lives here. Most requests are for healing various ailments. Warts. Leprosy. Toenail fungus."

Her eyebrows rose. "Skin lesions?"

Ah. It seemed they were done with pleasantries. "I've no idea what causes it."

Only a partial lie, but it wasn't like he could hand her the frog. The blasted critter had leapt from his workbench and disappeared into the tropical plants and vines that grew in his greenhouse. He'd searched for hours—days, weeks, months— but had never seen the creature again. He cancelled all visitations to his greenhouse, all the tours he'd promised of the strange, wonderful plants he'd shipped home, unwilling to expose another person to its bite. Now he was a recluse, fast becoming the village eccentric.

Unfortunately, forbidding anyone to enter his greenhouse had the opposite effect, generating ludicrous rumors that he'd brought home man-eating plants and snakes that could swallow a child whole. Soon adventure-seeking boys had arrived, peering through the condensation-fogged glass, trying to catch a glimpse of whatever lay hidden inside.

He'd ordered a lock—the 3XR CinchBolt—but it arrived too late. A little over a week ago, Evan awoke to find the door to his greenhouse ever so slightly ajar, the plants nearest the crack struggling to endure the cold spring morning.

Though nothing obvious had been stolen, his first thought had been of that blue frog. Had it escaped? It seemed so. For not three days later, Miss Tegan Price had knocked on his front door, begging an ointment for a strange rash. This time, she'd not been pretending an illness.

Plying Tegan with questions, he'd discovered that the frog had bitten her while she walked upon the foot path that led to his front door. After compounding a jar of ointment and sending her home with promises to call on her soon, he'd searched the path, the shrubs lining it, turning over every rock and fallen log he could reach, until finally resigning himself to failure. Instead, he turned to the desperate hope that the tropical frog had perished with the early morning's frost.

But he couldn't be certain. And now Piyali was here—the last place he wanted her.

"I owe you an apology," he said, speaking past the lump that blocked his throat. "I wanted to write... but things changed. I'm not the same man I was when I left." A gross understatement. He wasn't sure exactly what he was anymore, but according to the folklore the *Kayapo* shaman had shared, eventually he would no longer be human. Myth? He hoped so, but he couldn't be certain. With Tegan now facing the same fate...

"Did you meet someone?" Hurt shaded her voice as she searched his face. "Another woman?"

"No." His hand rose, reaching for her, but he forced it back to his side. "There will never be another woman for me, Piyali. I'm simply... unfit."

"An injury?" She glanced at his groin.

Blood rushed to his face, and he nearly choked. "Not that."

"Then what?" She placed a hand upon his arm, sending a fierce jolt of hunger through his body. "What is it that you feel you can't tell me? Once we shared... everything."

His eyes fell upon her rosy lips. He wanted nothing more than to pull her soft curves against his chest, to thread his fingers through the curls of her midnight-black hair that seemed to shine with its own light and pull her mouth to his. Kissing her would solve everything. And nothing.

The air between them shimmered with memories. At a fateful symposium—*Herbal Extracts and Their Use in the Treatment of Parasitic Infestations*—held at the Pharmacological Society of London, he'd lost awareness of all women but one. The attraction had been mutual, and a courtship had begun. Shared glances, touches, whispers over the course of several lectures, all culminating one fateful day in the shadowy recesses of the society's cloakroom. His pulse jumped at the memory of his mouth moving over her smooth skin, of linen and silk sliding to the ground, of her legs wrapped about his hips urging him closer, deeper.

He'd proposed the very next day on bended knee, asking her to come with him to South America. But her own dream had become reality, and with tears in her eyes, she showed him an acceptance letter granting her admission to medical school. In Paris.

Unwilling to let her go, he'd promised to ask her again in four years and begged her to wait for him.

Looking now into the twin dark pools of her eyes, he knew that with a few words, with a simple touch, she could be his once more. But at what cost? Her career. Possibly her life. He'd given her an apology, but he could not give her an explanation. Under no circumstances could he allow the British government to become aware of what had transpired. Nor would he inflict his future upon her.

The air was thick with regrets, making it hard to breathe.

"Evan?"

He dragged his eyes away, forcing himself to study the dappled light that filtered through the leaves above the surface of the spring. "You saw something through the aetheroscope," he said. "If it's not a fungal infection, the ointment I compounded won't cure her. Perhaps you ought to excise the lesion."

"Perhaps." Piyali moved out of reach, her boots tapping softly across the stepping stones. "Her skin, the basal layer, is blue. While that's odd enough, it also color shifted when I changed the angle of illumination." She lowered herself onto the low wall beside the water. "I've sent a skeet pigeon to London requesting my laboratory to send a replacement aetheroscope lens without delay. Before I set a course of treatment, I want to collect more data."

"Why not simply excise the lesion?" he asked, hoping she didn't find his insistence too presumptuous.

"Excision would prevent its spread, but once removed, the tissue—and anything that has invaded it—will die."

Exactly as he hoped. But she intended to investigate. Already, she'd dispatched a skeet pigeon to London. As his plans crumbled before him, Evan struggled to present her with a blank face. So much for his hopes of sending Piyali back to London without a sample. Still, if he could locate that blue frog, this disaster could be contained.

"Bet I can catch it first!"

"I'm faster!"

With a shout and a laugh, two boys ran up the pathway, skittering to a stop in the leaf litter at his feet.

"Simon," Evan greeted one boy, then the other. "Aron. Glad to see the skin's clearing up." He glanced at Piyali and murmured, "I've written a paper and plan to send my findings to the Pharmacological Society soon." They'd have to publish it, for he wouldn't be speaking in public.

The boy yanked his collar away from his neck. "Almost all gone," he said. "And no more itching." His face twisted as he stuck out his tongue. "But the tea is... blech."

Piyali stood and nodded a greeting. "Pleased to meet you both." She peered at the boy's face and neck, both impressed and incredulous. "You found a treatment for eczema?"

"From a shaman in the rainforest," Aron answered, his eyes wide and sparkling.

"If you're already cured," Piyali replied with a smile, "what brings you to the fairy well?"

"Mr. Tredegar told us all about how the natives hunt in the rainforest. With blow guns and poison darts," Aron said, snapping a branch off a nearby tree, whittling its end into a sharp point. "We're gonna do the same, soon as we find that blue frog."

"A blue frog," Piyali said. "What a coincidence." Her voice told him she knew it was anything but.

Biting back a curse, Evan closed his eyes. The creature's skin secretions might not be poisonous—not like the boys foolishly hoped—but its bite was a different matter. He had to catch that frog. Now.

CHAPTER THREE

Evan had bundled her back toward the tavern, reaching its door just as the sun slipped over the horizon. He'd refused to enter, refused to discuss the frog situation, muttering something about stoking the greenhouse stove as he turned away.

Bewildered, she stood there in the street as his form disappeared into the twilight. That he'd found an effective treatment for eczema was... amazing. Test, analyze, report. Since his return from Brazil, he'd sent a number of groundbreaking reports to the Pharmacological Society of London, and its members were all enamored of him. When this paper arrived, they would extend him a speaking invitation, but given he'd yet to visit London, she doubted he'd accept.

Was it because she lived in London? Or did it have something to do with this frog?

He'd almost kissed her there by the spring. She'd read the intent in his eyes. Dark and intense, it was the same stare he'd fastened upon her that first day their eyes caught in the lecture theater. Not the stare of hostility most women who dared step into the male stronghold received, but one of intrigued attraction. One he'd underscored by taking a chair beside her own. Then, as now, desire had rushed like liquid heat throughout her entire body.

If there was interest, was there still hope? Possibly. But this infection—and apparently a frog—stood between them. Love thwarted by an amphibian. Absurd.

Stomach growling, she stepped into the smoky tavern, hoping Sarah might be inclined to indulge in a bit of gossip. Perhaps she might know something about this elusive frog. Alas, she was busy carrying pints of ale and side-stepping the wandering hands of men who believed a compliment was best delivered by pinching a woman's rear. That they dared to do so in her father's presence said something about the man, casting him in a most unpleasant light. A father ought to defend his daughter's honor, *consistently.*

Among this cohort of men, one particular set of eyes with an arrogant gleam turned in Piyali's direction as she strode to the bar—back straight and chin held high—but the man's vanity refused to recognize her discouraging demeanor. His mouth widened in a manner suggestive of all kinds of improprieties as he rose from his chair.

A woman alone. An Indian woman alone. A young Indian woman in a skirt with a hemline that exposed her booted ankles... and escorted by no man.

Somehow this was an invitation. Once, such blatant interest unsettled her. Now, she viewed it as an opportunity to realign his priorities.

As he approached, his gaze shifted downward, raking over her body with an air of speculation, and she pulled back the edge of her overcoat, giving him a glimpse of her government issued TTX pistol in its holster. *That* snapped his drifting eyes back to a more acceptable location, and he dropped back into his chair, scowling. A most gratifying response. She allowed herself a small smile.

"Hungry?" the innkeeper asked as she settled onto a stool. "Got stew and Welsh rarebit."

"Rabbit?" she asked, her brow wrinkling.

A long-suffering sigh escaped his mouth. "Cheese on toast."

She could see the stew bubbling on the stove. Gristly beef and overcooked rutabagas in a fatty broth. Her throat constricted in protest, and her stomach also threatened to rebel. "The rarebit, please. And," she stopped him as he turned away, "the skeet pigeon?"

"Liftoff went as expected." He raised a shoulder and stepped aside as his wife slammed a pint of frothy, overflowing ale onto the bar before Piyali.

"Don't even think of drawing your weapon in my establishment," Mrs. Parker warned with narrowed eyes. "Next steamstage leaves at sunrise."

"I need to keep the room a few more days," Piyali said, ignoring the unnecessarily strong hint. "Bit of a problem with a frog, I'm afraid." She leaned forward eyeing the bandage wrapped about Mrs. Parker's fingers. "Is it infected?" Recalling Sarah's reaction to her mother's visit to the fairy well, and Evan's comments about offerings to the water-sprite, she added, "Did the bent pin you stuck yourself with happen to be rusted?"

Mrs. Parker stiffened. "What do you know about Seren's Well?"

"I know much about many things, such as a duck is a useful fowl. That two boys are on the hunt for a blue frog."

"Blue?" The innkeeper snorted, setting a plate of rarebit before her. "That's but a fairy tale to go with a fairy well." He gave his wife a hard stare. "What were you doing out there? Dipping your fingers in the sacred waters to rid yourself of warts?"

With a glare, his wife turned on her heel, tossing a few final words over her shoulder, "Keep it up, old man, and you'll find yourself outside sleeping in the steam cart."

Sarah leaned close as she passed behind Piyali. "See why I'm so desperate to marry? It's a rare moment they're ever in agreement about anything. But what's this about a blue frog?"

So much for her source of gossip.

H er mind unsettled, Piyali tossed and turned all night on the lumpy mattress and, by morning, she was convinced it was stuffed with hay—not feathers—and infested by creepy-crawlies with an inclination to bite. She'd had sleepless nights before, but always—even in Paris—her fingers had been able to trace the embroidered motifs of her *kantha* quilt, the various flowers and birds stitched into the fabric by her *dida's* very own fingers. During such restless nights, she allowed herself to remember a very different life, one she'd lost long ago. Such memories were the force that drove her to study infectious disease.

Before the sun had fully crept over the horizon, she was dressed—this time in a subtle coppery-orange *lehenga*—and pacing the rough boards of her room. A mythical fairy well, a blue frog and two boys on a quest to locate it in the undergrowth surrounding the pool. All had sounded like nonsense until Evan had turned her around and marched her away from said spring as fast as their feet would carry them, a muscle jumping in his clenched jaw.

Grounds for further investigation.

She glanced at the pocket watch that hung from her corset on a silver chain. The general store would be open by now. Miss Price, pampered daughter though she was, might be minding the counter with her mother. Perhaps if Piyali could draw her aside, she might coax forth more details.

With a quick check of her TTX pistol—men waking from a drunken stupor were often irate—she shrugged on her overcoat, picked up her doctor's bag and stepped from her room. She exited the tavern into the cool, fresh air that promised a beautiful spring day.

"I'm Dr. Mukherji, here to check on your daughter," she said, nodding a greeting to Mr. Price as she entered the store. He stood behind a gleaming brass till, tying on an apron as he prepared for the day's business.

"Heard about you." Mr. Price stared back at her, his eyes flat and unwelcoming. "Heard you were a woman. Trained in Paris, no less."

Would she always be greeted with such venom? Quite probably. Not that she would let that stop her. She pulled back her shoulders and met his gaze directly. "With a specialty in infectious diseases." She stood silent, letting that detail sink in, waiting to see if he was prejudiced enough that he would risk his daughter's health.

His jaw slackened. "Is it…"

"I've no idea," she answered, happy to have his complete attention, his grudging respect. "But I want to monitor her condition carefully."

Miss Price was presented without delay.

In a snit, Tegan flounced into the room. "This isn't necessary," she whined. "Mr. Tredegar is a renowned pharmacist."

"So he is," Piyali agreed, quietly wondering if anything more than the promise of financial security drove her interest in Evan. "But all men and women of science consult their colleagues. What two minds can accomplish together is far more than the sum of their individual work."

"Sit," her father commanded.

With a huff, Tegan sat upon a nearby chair.

Piyali knelt to unwind the gauze from Tegan's ankle. Much to her relief, the blue lesion didn't appear to have spread. Neither, however, had it decreased in size. Perhaps Evan's ointment had had some effect. Except, without an untreated lesion for comparison, no true scientific conclusion could be reached. Not that this was something she wished to test on a young woman. Or any other person.

"Where in the woods were you bitten?" If she could catch the creature, the minute her lens arrived she could analyze its saliva beneath her aetheroscope.

Tegan shrugged. "On a path." But her eyes slid away.

Piyali dropped her voice to a mere murmur. "Might this unfortunate event have occurred beside Seren's Well?" A soft gasp from her patient. "The location of the attack—" A frog attacking. The very phrase sounded ludicrous. "Shall remain between us. Doctor-patient confidentiality."

"You—an outsider—have no business at our fairy well." Tegan crossed her arms and pursed her lips. "Who told you about it? No. Let me guess. Sarah. She'd do anything to win."

"Win?" What on earth could the spring have to do with the two women's matrimonial designs upon Evan?

"Don't pretend you don't know," Tegan huffed. "Your flashy dress and exotic, dark looks might draw Evan's glances, but he won't marry you." The spiteful use of his given name was not lost upon her, and it stung, the implication she was nothing but a pretty plaything to be used and tossed aside. "You wouldn't fit in. Not here. What he needs is a true Welsh woman to look after him."

Tegan thought her the newest competitor for Evan's romantic attentions. While Sarah had all but welcomed her to join the game, Tegan refused her admission outright. Yet once, Evan had asked Piyali to share his life. Not so these village girls, not even after months of shameless pursuit. "You'd rather lose a limb than confide the location of the frog?"

Hard eyes glinted at her and, when she spoke, her voice was hushed, staking an intimate claim. "If you *must* know, I was bitten on the path just outside Evan's front door whilst returning from our usual rendezvous." Her patient leaned closer. "We have spent time together behind closed doors. Frequently. His mother's opal and diamond ring *will* be mine."

That did it. She would not tolerate such disrespect. Slamming shut her bag, she stood. She was under no obligation to coddle Tegan's misguided hopes. And so Piyali left her there, perched like a queen upon her throne, to reapply Evan's *miraculous* ointment on her own.

Striding down the street, fingers clenched about the handle of her bag, Piyali searched the edge of the woods, hunting for a break in the vegetation, for the path that would lead her to Seren's Well. Either Tegan was lying or the frog had hopped through the woods until it found a likely location to establish a new home. She would find it, and she would analyze it, dragging it back to London as her small, blue hostage if necessary. With or without Evan's approval.

Evan. Good grief. Sarah and Tegan were poised to claw each other's eyes out over the man. But neither of the young woman knew—or cared—anything of his heart. Tegan wanted nothing but economic security attached to a handsome man. Sarah wanted all that and escape from her parents with the promise of a touch of adventure.

Piyali wanted him for himself.

Yes, Evan's physique was impressive. Particularly after spending four years deep in the rainforest. He had sharper edges now. His body was tougher, harder, as if his muscles were forged from steel. She couldn't help but wonder what it would feel like—now—to be wrapped in his strong arms. His gray-blue eyes held a depth that hadn't been there before, and yet his gaze still sent blue flames ablaze across her skin. Yet she craved more than his physical touch. She missed his impressive mind, his advanced thinking, his adventurous spirit, his kindness, his directness... though that last trait now seemed lacking.

She sighed. He was holding something close to his chest and—setting aside her hurt, anger, jealousy, and disappointment—she was nearly certain he was trying to protect her. She frowned. But from a frog?

Her eye caught upon a break in the underbrush. The packed dirt of a path. She ducked beneath a branch and entered the forest.

Whatever ate at Evan's conscience, it must be serious, or even now his ring would be on her finger. Opal and diamond. His mother's ring. The ring he'd presented her on bended knee all those years ago. She'd wanted to accept, to announce to all the world that they would be husband and wife. But the dreams they both pursued were about to drag them into separate hemispheres for four long years. Any number of things could happen to drive a wedge between them.

And, indeed, something had.

Evan had nearly caught the blasted amphibian twice. The first time he'd been too slow, the second time his net had snagged upon the underbrush. Half the night he'd sat awake upon the cold, hard stone wall, staring into the bubbling spring. Pointing his bioluminescent torch at one likely crevice after another, he'd tried to search out the wee beastie's new home. Then, like an ember jumping from a freshly stoked furnace, it struck him hot and burning between the eyes. He was an idiot.

Tree frog.

He'd turned the beam of his torch upward, searching the overhanging branches. The frog must have been snoozing comfortably, tucked within a cluster of dew-damp leaves, for it wasn't until the first rays of sunlight fell upon the leaf canopy that he caught a glimpse of something blue and shimmery.

Scaling the tree, he wriggled out onto the branch, holding the handle of his net tightly as he stretched his arm ever so slowly and carefully toward the frog. But despite his stealth, the amphibian turned about, blinked at him—once, twice—then launched itself into the pool.

Grumbling about frogs and trans-Atlantic voyages to vacation at a mineral spring in Wales, Evan dropped back to the ground. The cold shock of the water must have been too much, for the critter now hopped about in the weeds edging the water. Evan lunged, almost catching him.

Now the blue frog was somewhere between the stones of the low wall. On hands and knees, he crawled through dew-damp grass, peering into one crack after another.

"Much as I can appreciate the posterior view you present," Piyali said behind him, her voice full of smothered laughter, "wouldn't it be easier to admit you need help catching a certain blue frog?"

Evan scrambled to his feet, nearly pitching himself into the pool in his haste. He dragged a gloved hand over his hair, then cursed silently, remembering he'd just been on all fours in the dirt. Closing his eyes a moment, he swallowed his pride. It was for the greater good. "Will you help me?"

"Fine." She set down her bag and picked up a long stick. "But if I find him first, I won't share unless you tell me what's going on."

"No." Absolutely not. Under no circumstances could the frog be allowed to leave Aberwyn. The poor creature would have to be destroyed.

"No?" she scoffed, poking into a crevice. "You'd rather see the frog dragged back to London, poked, prodded, its every secret extracted? That lesion of Miss Price's? Still there, your ointment notwithstanding. What becomes of her if I don't discover the cause of her skin infection?"

"The lesion needs to be excised," he stated. The ointment would only slow the spread of the discoloration, not eliminate it. Better a doctor perform the surgery, but if necessary he would lift a scalpel and do his best.

"Oh?" She threw a challenging glance over her shoulder. "What brings you to that conclusion? Such a surgery risks an infection of another kind."

The sunlight filtering through the leaves overhead accentuated her thick eyelashes, the curve of her cheek and the graceful arch of her neck. *The pistol at her hip.* She was a Queen's agent now. Even if he told her everything, her loyalty was to Britain first, him... at best, second.

But if he didn't tell her, she was going to keep digging. If that frog bit her... if what had happened to him, happened to her... His gut twisted. He couldn't bear it. She could help. Together, they might just be able to solve—

The air shimmered. Odd. Nothing sat there upon the rock wall. Or did it? He swept his net across its surface and felt something catch in the mesh. A small weight, about that of a small, shimmering tree frog. Quickly, he tied off the opening.

"Did you catch it?" Piyali asked, crossing to him to stare into his net. "There's nothing—"

There was. Tiny and thrashing and barely visible, the once-blue frog reflected the light of the forest around them. A near-perfect camouflage. No wonder he'd had such a difficult time locating the creature.

"I've a glass terrarium," he announced, partly to her, party to the frog. "No more hopping about biting the ankles of young women."

"Evan," Piyali's voice was soft as she wrapped a hand about his wrist. "You have to tell me what's going on. Don't make me summon Mr. Black."

"Mr. Black," he repeated. He'd met the man only once, but once had been enough to cement the man in his mind. If Mr. Black was involved, the situation was worse than he thought. "He sent you?"

"He did. I'm to solve the mystery of the blue lesion and evaluate your competence."

"For?" Worry twisted in his stomach.

With a deep breath, she dropped an artillery shell, exploding his calm resignation to his fate. "Mr. Ranunculus has taken ill and is not expected to recover. They're searching for a new Director of Tropical Plants to work in the Lister Botanical Gardens and Greenhouse. Your name was put forth."

"Mine." The depth of resources they possessed alone was enough to turn his head. To be a member of that institution—one that collected the greatest minds and the most obscure botanical specimens from all over the globe—would be an honor. To become one of its directors? He hardly dared hope they would ever consider him. His pulse jumped despite the impossibility.

Piyali shifted closer and the silver, metallic threads sewn into her bright skirt shimmered. Only then did he realize how overdressed she was for a walk in the woods. The moment he'd met her, his life had exploded into vibrant color. Without her, the intensity had slowly washed away... until now. He yearned to accept the offer, both her unspoken one and the directorship.

"I'm told your papers on the medicinal value of Brazilian flora are groundbreaking," Piyali cajoled.

They were, but he would never pass the interview process. They would note his reluctance to remove his gloves, to dig into the dirt with bare hands. No, he'd not be offered the position. Instead, he would find himself installed in the biological research laboratories as a specimen himself.

His stomach churned. He could not allow them to discover his secret. Notes scribbled as the shaman spoke about the curse indicated that Evan had a year. Perhaps two. In that time he needed to make arrangements for the support of his sister and grandmother, to explore the medicinal properties of the eighty-one novel plants he'd so carefully transported to Wales. To publish his results. He would not survive the intense scrutiny of Lister Laboratories.

As if she read his mind, Piyali said, "I'm afraid the clamor for one particular pharmacobotanist is loud. If you refuse, they may insist."

Imagining an entire suit-clad committee arriving in Aberwyn to inspect both him and his greenhouse painted a grim picture. His secret would be discovered. Better to trust one particularly insistent Lister University physician. He barked a laugh. Was defeat inevitable? "Come then, Piyali. Grab your bag."

CHAPTER FOUR

The moment Piyali entered the greenhouse, humidity began to curl the tendrils of hair that had escaped her braid during the frog hunt. Moisture gathered at her temples. "It's amazing."

She'd stepped into a traditional Welsh cottage of stone, through the large room—kitchen and living space—barely taking note of a large desk stacked with texts and papers, of a table and shelves covered with glassware and plant cuttings and chemicals. She'd hurried through to the back of the cottage, intent upon seeing the greenhouse Evan had described when they'd strolled the streets of London beneath the moonlight, speaking to each other of their pasts, of their hopes to balance careers and family in the future.

Slowly she turned about, staring in amazement. Great sheets of glass supported by an iron framework let in the fading beams of afternoon sunlight, and in the center, a leviathan of a stove burned large blocks of peat, churning out heat, intent upon defying the chill of a Welsh spring day. All about her, trees stretched their branches upward as vine upon vine twisted about their trunks, also stretching toward the sun. Exotic bushes and shrubby plants covered every inch of the ground, all but a narrow walkway that meandered between them. It was a lush, tropical paradise. Particularly as it came without the usual accompaniment of biting insect life. Her enthusiasm was dampened only by the knowledge that this must be where the blue frog with the toxic bite originated.

"It's far more wonderful than you ever described." She reached out with gentle fingers to stroke the soft petals of a beautiful, orange flower.

Catching her fingers, Evan shook his head in warning. "This one is safe. But remember my assignment was to collect potent flora. Not everything here is harmless, even to touch."

"Much like its curator." Her heart jumped as her eyes fell on his rumpled cravat, and her fingers ached with the memory of the last time she'd untangled its knot, pulling on its loose ends to bring his lips to hers. Did she dare? She lifted her gaze to his face. The corners of his mouth twitched with a suppressed smile. Progress.

"You smell of orange blossoms." His gloved fingertip touched the glass vial that hung from a loop on her corset. "You kept it."

Now was the time to revisit the past, before darker topics stole the moment. "Always," she said, moving closer to rest her palm against the hard plane of his chest. "It's my favorite scent. Ever since you gave me my first vial and informed me it was an aphrodisiac." She tipped her face upward. "Is it working?"

"Too well." His gloved hand tightened about hers. "It's driving me insane."

"Once you wouldn't hesitate." They'd shared stolen kisses in shadowed alcoves at any and every opportunity. She walked her fingers up his chest. "What happened? What could possibly be so awful that you would rather chase me away than confide in me, a woman you once asked to share your life?"

"Piyali," he growled. "I can't make promises anymore."

"I'm not asking for one." She slid her hand over the rough stubble of his cheek, its rasp triggering a flood of cherished memories. "Just a confidence, perhaps a kiss."

Something deep inside him seemed to snap. Cupping the base of her skull with both hands, he dropped his lips to hers. Soft, warm, sweet. A gentle kiss that spoke of a longing ache finally satisfied. Then she parted her lips and reminded him that for too long, their hunger, their thirst for each other had gone unsatisfied.

His tongue dove into her mouth, devouring her, consuming her. Wrapping her arms about his waist, she pulled him closer, moaning encouragement as she pressed her breasts tight to his chest until she could feel his heart pounding.

Sparks flew. Five long years with an ocean between them. Not a single man compared to Evan. Not one of the many men who once pursued her had managed to hide his horror at the idea of a working wife. Not one had eyes that saw into her soul, causing her breath to catch, her heart to race in anticipation. *This* was why she'd waited.

"God, I've missed you," Evan rasped as his mouth left her lips, trailing kisses along her jaw, her neck, sending shivers across her skin and a rush of warmth between her thighs. He slid his hands down her back to fall on her hips, yanking her tight against his own. Whatever it was that had kept him from her, it wasn't a lack of attraction, for there was *firm* evidence of that.

Encouraged, she smiled against his neck. "We've waited forever," she whispered, "to be alone like this." She nibbled his earlobe. "Perhaps we could try a bed this time?"

A low rumble sounded in his chest. "Piyali, it's near impossible to refuse you."

"Then don't."

His hands loosened on her hips as he took a step backward, refusing to lift his eyes to meet hers. "We can't. Not until—"

A loud knock sounded, and his head swiveled. Piyali wanted to scream in frustration. Not merely because she wanted to explore the advantages of a feather mattress with Evan, but because he'd been about to tell her what was wrong. If she knew what was broken, perhaps she could make repairs. She caught the edge of his chin in her palm. "Tell me. Until what?"

More knocking, this time louder and more frantic. "Mr. Tredegar!"

"Don't," she pleaded even as he turned toward the door connecting the greenhouse to the more traditional Welsh cottage.

"It's Tegan," he said. Regret softened his voice. "I can't ignore her. The frog bite, it's my fault. Or perhaps there's been some injury to another within the village... Stay here. Don't let her see you."

Her face burned. "I won't have what's between us hidden away, Evan. Not this time."

"I'm not ashamed," he said. "I never was. But she's a spiteful girl, always has been. Would you have the whole village know of our past before we sort out if there's to be a future? It would compromise your entire investigation."

Bang. Bang. "Evan!"

His fault. He'd said the frog bite was his fault. "You'll tell me everything?" she asked.

His mouth opened, then closed. "I promise."

For all that was worth.

Managing a tight nod, she conceded his point. "Fine." She spun on her heel and moved deeper into the foliage, hiding like a shameful secret.

Evan opened the front door, and Tegan pushed past him, stomping into the small cottage. "What can I do for you, Miss Price?"

"A headache powder for Mrs. Lewis," she answered, pacing about the room, stopping before his worktable to stare at the miscellaneous equipment—flasks, alcohol burners, glass distillation tubing, among others—gathered together, along with a number of various compounds extracted from tropical plants, ready for his next experiment. She waved at a mortar and pestle. "No, make that two." Tegan pressed her hands to her temples.

Worry flared. He closed the distance between them to study her face. She seemed rather flushed, her eyes shadowed. What if the infection had spread to her blood? "Are you sick? Feverish? Does your ankle pain you?"

"I'm fine." She waved a hand. "What pains me are the games we play, Evan."

A whisper of worry snaked its way down his spine at the use of his given name. Rouge, not fever colored her cheeks and lips—and was that coal dust upon her eyelashes? Immediately, he regretted unlatching the door. "Games?" he repeated. "Miss Price, this is most improper."

"It wouldn't be improper," Tegan fluttered her eyelashes in what must be an attempt at seduction, but only served to remind him that she was barely old enough for long skirts, "if you'd drop to one knee and offer that opal ring to me."

He bit back a curse. "I—"

"I know you intend to offer for me." She lifted her face. "You've been so patient, so solicitous of my fragile health, rushing to my side with a special ointment when that awful creature assaulted me in the woods."

The bite of a frog was an assault? It sounded ridiculous, but given how the blue blemish would spread...

A strangled snort from the greenhouse had him reaching for Tegan's shoulder to steer her away from its entrance. "I'm sorry, Miss Price, if I've given you the wrong impression, but—"

"I'll make you the perfect wife, Evan." She lunged, flinging herself at him, and he was forced to catch the girl in his arms. "We shall run the most prosperous pharmacy in all of Cardiff. The sooner the banns are read, the sooner we can be together."

Aether, he'd sorely misjudged the love-sick glances she'd tossed him, chalking them up to a youthful infatuation that would pass. Gripping both of her shoulders firmly, he pushed her away. "I've no plans to marry. We cannot be together. You ought to go now, unless you still require headache powders?"

Her eyes filled with tears. *Tears!* How could he fix this?

"No," she sniffled. "No powders. Unless you've one for heartache?"

"Er."

Tegan ran for the door, flinging it wide. "When you realize your mistake, I'll be waiting. Waiting for you." With that dramatic aside, she ran from his cottage into the woods.

Strangled laughter burst from the greenhouse. Two dark eyes peeked around the door frame. "Oh you cruel, cruel man. How could you turn down such an impassioned plea?"

"Not funny." He ran a hand over the back of his stiff neck. "How am I to ever present myself at the town store again? Let alone examine her lesion?"

"You won't have to." Piyali glanced about as she stepped into the one large room that served as kitchen, living space and laboratory. What must she think of his primitive cottage? Of the uneven flagstones upon the floor, the cast iron stove crammed into an ancient hearth, little furniture beyond a desk, a rough wooden table and chairs? "I'll examine her lesion," she said. "And you need not stay in Wales. I hear there's a position available for a pharmacobotanist in London. That it's practically his for the asking."

She looked at him from beneath long eyelashes, and his mind flashed to his thick, feather mattress. There was nothing he'd rather do more than slide an engagement ring onto Piyali's finger, carry her upstairs to his bed. Then leave with her for London on a hunt for a special license followed by a visit to Mr. Black to accept the invitation to interview. Once she saw his hand, however… His stomach hurt as if he'd swallowed a solution of quicksilver salts.

Two paths lay before him.

Refuse to confide in her, and Piyali would summon Mr. Black. That would bring him under intense and unwanted scrutiny. It would, however, leave him time to excise Tegan's lesion and destroy the frog.

Or he could reveal his secret and beg for her help and silence. He lifted his eyes to meet her watchful gaze. Trained at the Université de Paris in infectious diseases, handed her own laboratory at Lister University and recruited to the Queen's agents, she was an expert in her field. If anyone could solve the mystery, he had no doubt it would be her.

He gave a stiff nod and, eyeing the terrarium where a certain shimmering frog crouched, tugged off his leather gloves. First the left—nothing unusual to see there—and then the right.

"It's blue!" Piyali gasped. "Your hand, the entire thing. Blue!"

That was the color of the moment. He rolled back the cuff of his shirtsleeves.

"Schistosomiasis!" Her hands clapped over her mouth as her impossibly wide eyes took in the disaster that had transpired. "How far has it spread?"

"Far," he said, yanking off his cravat and unbuttoning his collar. He tugged it aside so she could see how its tendrils crept across his shoulder toward the base of his neck.

"Does it hurt?" Her hand darted forward, then stopped, fluttering, uncertain if she should touch.

"No." Not physically. The anguish was entirely mental. "The infection is completely painless. A tiny bite by our tiny blue nemesis, and the next day I awoke with a lesion a half-inch in diameter. A day later, one inch. It had encompassed my entire hand and wrist by the time I compounded an ointment—the one I shared with Miss Price—that slowed its progress."

"Slowed," she repeated. Grief and heartache mingled on her face.

"So far I've only managed to delay the inevitable. There's a myth among the natives I studied with, it translates roughly as the 'Tribe of Invisible Devils'. Once bitten by the blue—sometimes invisible—frog, the curse overtakes the body, one limb at a time. Legend claims that when the disease consumes them, madness sends a man—or a woman—running into the rainforest never to be seen again. Many choose to take their lives rather than face that fate."

"And when it... consumes the entire body?" Piyali pressed a shaking hand to her throat as the full implications of his situation registered.

"Banishment." Wisps of a black fog began to cloud his mind as he stared down at his hand, at this now alien piece of himself. It was a daily struggle to reconcile himself to his future. "They can't allow a man—or woman—to remain within the tribe because with extreme or heightened emotion, the skin begins to glimmer, to color-shift and reflect the world about it."

"Making him—or her—invisible."

She had a beautiful, quick mind. "Exactly. And the tribe won't tolerate something it can't see. Ghosts. Devils. Call them what you will, they can no longer be a member of society. That is my fate. And the reason we can't marry. I may last a year, two." He lifted a shoulder, not wanting to upset her further by revealing his distress. "Perhaps five. But once the blue crawls up my neck, I'll no longer be fit for British society."

"Can I touch it—you?" she asked, reaching out again. "Is it contagious?"

"If it were, I'd never have allowed you to examine Miss Price." He held out his hand.

She cupped it gently in her palm, turning it over to study it from all angles. Determination injected steel into her voice. "I'll find a way to fix this. We'll find a cure. Together."

Hope had long since died. It lay, black and shriveled in a dusty, forgotten place. All that was left was to save others from a similar fate. He kissed her on her forehead, then dropped the other shoe. "You can't tell Mr. Black."

Jerking back, she released his hand, taking away the comforting warmth of her touch. He dared not reach for her. Not now. Emotion needed to be set aside. "But—"

"Imagine what Britain would do with such knowledge. Men—agents—would be purposefully infected, sent across borders. God forbid the technique fall into enemy hands. All because a small, blue frog hitched a ride on one of my plants. I'm begging you, Piyali. Better to destroy the frog and leave me—and Miss Price—to our ends."

"Ends..." Wrapping her arms across her chest, she shook her head, unwilling to accept such a scenario. "It could take years. How do you propose to cope as whatever this is overtakes the both of you?"

"Excision of her lesion would be my first choice. Failing that, I could marry her." Tegan would find it a bitter life. There'd be no romance, no pharmacy in Cardiff, no social interactions of any kind. Eventually, even her family would not be able to visit. "Hide her from society. You heard her, she's amenable and already considered in fragile health."

Piyali's mouth tightened. "Yet you declined her."

"I did." Tegan was a constant thorn in his side. The only woman he *wished* to marry was Piyali. "But if it saves lives..."

"Unacceptable," Piyali cut off his words. If anyone was to marry him, it ought to be her. How dare he suggest such steps? Tegan's overt manipulations had been amusing until Evan raised it as a feasible option. But such messy emotions must be shoved aside; there was no time for them. They needed to take advantage of every moment left. "I refuse to abandon you to an uncertain fate."

She spun on her heel to face the scarred wooden table that served as his workbench and studied his makeshift laboratory. A scale. Boxes and jars and tin containers filled with powders and oils and emollients. Bottles and flasks. Tubing and corks. All manner of titration and distillation equipment. An excellent chemistry setup, but not conducive to microbiology.

Evan followed her and began to clear one end of the table, his features set in stone. "Tell me what you need. If it's not here, I'll find it."

She thought of the frog inside the terrarium. Calm, in safe and secure surroundings, it had returned to its lustrous blue color. She *had* to find a cure; the alternative was unacceptable. Gears spun in her mind. If infection was transmitted through a bite, that meant the contagion was contained within its saliva.

Ducking into the greenhouse, she retrieved her black bag and dug into it, pulling out a number of glass aetheroscope slides and cotton-tipped sticks. "To begin, we'll need to swab the inside of the frog's mouth— and biopsy its skin. Given its camouflage capabilities, I suspect the amphibian harbors the infectious agent throughout its entire body."

"I'll do that," Evan stated. "Carefully. While wearing heavy gloves."

So like him, always looking out for the welfare of others, putting her safety above his. But today it left a bitter taste in her mouth. If only he'd answered her message with the truth of his terrible situation. "I'll set up my aetheroscope here." She moved to the large desk, setting aside stacks of books and papers to claim a corner. "We'll also biopsy your skin. Near the initial bite, further up your arm so that we might see if cell morphology alters over the progression, over the spread of the disease. And for comparison to Tegan's biopsy."

"The broken objective?"

"Will hinder our progress." She pressed her lips together. Odds that Mr. Black would be able to send one in their direction any time soon were low. He'd made some quip about selkie trouble in the north and needing to travel to Scotland. His mission could take a day... or it could last for weeks, and she hated to leave Evan alone lest he take some drastic action. "Is there any chance of finding a replacement in Cardiff?"

"There is," Evan answered. "Today, we collect evidence and, tomorrow, we'll travel to Cardiff to gather necessary supplies?"

"Agreed."

Piyali turned away, her grip tightening upon the swab she held. Conflicting loyalties battled in her mind. In Cardiff, there would be reliable skeet pigeons to hire. As a Queen's agent, she was bound to report this development to Mr. Black, but what did she have beyond a fanciful tale of a rogue Amazonian frog prone to bite? Besides, this was Evan, and Mr. Black was likely still in Scotland. A few days of investigation would provide her with more data, more evidence. Her report could wait a few days.

CHAPTER FIVE

Piyali's wide smile set Mrs. Parker grumbling. Despite Evan's revelation, the prospect of spending a day at his side—this time in the open air and beneath the sunshine—had floated her mood into the upper aether, as if a curse placed upon them by some wart-nosed witch had lifted.

Yesterday, their heads together, they'd taken turns staring through her aetheroscope at slide after slide after slide, until their eyes began to cross. The frog's saliva provided no answers. No visible micro-organisms writhed or wriggled beneath their view at which they could point fingers. All skin biopsies appeared—more or less—the same. Including that of the frog.

Nonetheless, they'd set up a number of cultures, using what was available from Evan's meager bachelor's kitchen stores, in an attempt to coax any infectious agent to grow and multiply.

Piyali had a favored hypothesis, but until she could obtain a higher resolution with her aetheroscope, it was no better than wild speculation. If the organism responsible was intracellular, a replacement objective— along with a few additional specialized stains—would disclose its presence.

A grunt of irritation jerked her back to the moment, and a plate of oatcakes was slammed onto the table before her along with the tavern's ubiquitous ale. Mrs. Parker's expression suggested she hoped her breakfast guests would choke.

"For breakfast?" Piyali asked, eyeing the frothy, unfiltered drink.

"I suppose you're used to drinking *tea.*" Mrs. Parker snarled the last word as if the beverage derived from a chamber pot. With a sneer, she dropped a copper tea kettle onto the range with a loud clang. "We aim to serve."

"Well, yes. Thank you." It was then that Piyali noticed Mrs. Parker's bandage was no longer confined to her fingers. It now wrapped about the entirety of her hand. Moreover, she pressed her hand to her waist as if its use pained her. "Perhaps I should look at your injury?"

Mrs. Parker's answering glare vibrated with barely-suppressed hostility.

"Mother." Sarah's voice cajoled as she crossed the room, "let her look. She *is* a physician. If it's infected, her attentions are better than Father's." She rolled her eyes. "Though I'm certain he exaggerated when he offered to lop off your finger."

The villagers seemed overly concerned with amputation, though the Parkers needled each other at every possible opportunity. Why on earth they'd chosen to marry was beyond her comprehension.

"I'm sure amputation won't be necessary," Piyali began diplomatically, "but infections shouldn't be left untreated. Mr. Tredegar is a competent pharmacist, Mrs. Parker. Today we are traveling to Cardiff, to his store. If you require an antibacterial—"

"Cardiff?" Her eyebrows arched toward her hairline. "Together? Alone?"

"Yes," Piyali answered. "I'm in need of supplies."

"No. That will not do. Sarah, get your bonnet. You must accompany them for propriety's sake."

Sarah's eyes brightened, but she glanced at Piyali and demurred. "I don't think my company is desired, Mother."

"Nonsense." Mrs. Parker waved her bandaged hand and winced. "I'll draw up a list of required items." She strode away before any further objections could be voiced.

"I'm sorry," Sarah sighed. "She pressures me daily to win Mr. Tredegar's regard. I promise not to be too obnoxious. Would it help if I promise to make myself scarce once we arrive? There's a book I wish to purchase at the booksellers and—wafts of aether—what I wouldn't do to escape Mother if only for a day." A mischievous look lit her face, and she leaned close, adding in a conspiratorial whisper. "I have to admit Tegan's jealousy would sweeten the trip just that much more."

Only rigid determination kept Piyali's shoulders from slumping. To invite Sarah along meant hiding— yet again—her rekindling relationship with Evan. A relationship that wouldn't have a chance if they couldn't concoct a cure. She wanted time with him, but maintaining Sarah's friendship and good graces was important. Particularly as her mother had acquired her infection at the fairy well before the Amazonian frog was apprehended. How else would she be informed about village affairs? And she had to admit, she liked the young woman. "Very well," she conceded, "but only if you answer one question about your mother."

"Oh?" Sarah looked as if facing her mother's irritation might be preferable. "What is it you want to know?"

"Nothing much. I'm a physician and can't help but care." More she was curious. "Her wound, is it blue?"

"Blue?" Sarah's face scrunched up as she thought. "No, not exactly, but it is spreading rather quickly. Her skin has taken on a rather odd appearance. I only glimpsed it, but I'd say it was pink and shimmery. The wound itself has mostly healed."

That fit. Mrs. Parker was nearly always in a foul mood. Shimmery and pinkish when feelings ran strong.

"Is that what's wrong with Tegan?" Sarah leaned closer. "The reason you're here? Is she—for once—truly sick?" She gasped. "Don't tell me her ankle is *blue!*"

Secrets in a village. One in exchange for another. Sharing that information went against all her medical training, but not necessarily that of the Queen's agents. "Cultivate the locals" was one of Mr. Black's favorite expressions. She needed to play along. Besides, Sarah had guessed. Was it wrong that deep in a corner of her soul she was enjoying this moment?

Pressing a finger to her lips, Piyali too leaned forward. "*Shh.* I never said a thing. Don't let this become public knowledge."

"Sarah," Mrs. Parker bellowed. "Your bonnet. No daughter of mine shall freckle in the sun."

Sarah winked, then hurried to her mother's bidding.

A few minutes later, after forcing down a dry oatcake with weak tea, Piyali waited as Evan handed Sarah into the crank wagon. Resignation and reproach tugged his lips into a frown as he glanced at her sideways.

"I had to," she whispered, noting how Sarah sat in the middle of the rough board that formed a seat. "An exchange of favors." She pretended to stumble, bringing her mouth to Evan's ear. "She doesn't realize it, but her mother has also been bitten by the frog."

He cursed under his breath. "You have Sarah spying for you?"

"A necessary step," Piyali breathed back. "Mrs. Parker is refusing any and all treatment." She hesitated.

Much as she wished to dismiss this professional duty...
"We ought to check on Tegan."

"Already done," Evan replied, taking Piyali's medical bag to place it inside the cart. "Her condition remains unchanged. Now up, we've a long day ahead of us."

As they drove away, a curtain twitched, and Piyali caught a glimpse of Tegan's vexed face pressed to the window of the village store. Her pursuit of Evan was far from over.

T he road to Cardiff was rutted and rocky, and Sarah—who had planted herself between him and Piyali—took every advantage to bump against him. Shoulders, hips, legs. Even her hand slid from her lap to press the side of her pinky finger to his thigh. Evan supposed he ought to be grateful that she didn't outright climb into his lap. So much for enjoying the pleasant spring day with Piyali. His fault, he supposed, for refusing to reveal their relationship. From the amused press of her lips, she knew exactly what Sarah was up to. At least Miss Parker wasn't demanding a proposal.

Relationship. He swallowed hard. A mistake. But with that kiss, a seed of hope had germinated. The oppressive feeling of doom and gloom had lifted—ever so slightly—as he unburdened his secrets. Still, there was a lingering feeling of melancholy, a certain pessimism that even if they managed to uncover the cause of his infection, they wouldn't be able to formulate a treatment.

All night, he'd worried about bringing her into his confidence, not at all certain he had made the right choice. Now, with the unwelcome revelation that the frog had another victim, the situation threatened to grow out of hand.

He forced himself to listen to the women's chatter.

"What book are you hoping to find in Cardiff?" Piyali asked Sarah.

"Well, I'm not certain." Sarah fiddled with the ribbon at her chin. "Not exactly. Though I hope to find an intelligent husband," she fluttered her eyelashes at Evan, "I thought I might follow your example and become a self-sufficient, career-minded woman."

"Oh?" Piyali raised her eyebrows.

"I adore babies," Sarah said, then addressed her next comment to him. "While I work to convince a handsome, young man to start a family of his own," her eyelashes fluttered again, "I'm aiming to attend a woman's college. There's a school opening in Cardiff, and I mean to apply. Perhaps someday I might manage medical school. I hear there's an entire field of medicine involving childbirth— obstetrics and gynecology." Her brow wrinkled. "But first, I have to pass an entrance exam."

Evan cleared his throat. "Hence the bookstore."

"Yes. I won't keep you from your errands, but perhaps you might recommend a few titles?"

Piyali rattled off a few, and it brought a certain measure of relief to know that Sarah was taking control of her future, beyond plaguing him with endless flirtations and shameless suggestions. Even though his ears began to burn as the two women discussed childbirth with much candor and detail. He squirmed on his seat.

He dropped Sarah off at the booksellers—with great relief—before continuing to his own store. "Was that necessary?"

She smiled and fluttered her eyelashes in imitation of Sarah. "Better than discussing the making of babies, was it not?"

Now he could think of nothing else. Could his face grow any hotter?

Ears burning, he redirected the conversation. "I hope you don't mind, but I do have customers who will wish to consult a pharmacist. And, if you're willing, a physician."

"Of course."

They rattled to a stop behind his store. Several long weeks had passed since he'd last visited his sister and *mamgu*, his grandmother. It was hard making constant excuses for his gloves but, when the worst came to pass, the business must support them, and for that, more preparation would be required. Only when he had no choice but to confide in them, would he reveal his blue appendage.

The moment his sister Megan realized it was him, not some delivery cart, she rushed from the service door. "Evan!" she exclaimed, throwing her arms about him. "And who is this?" she asked, knowing damn well exactly who Piyali was.

He hugged his *mamgu*, then performed introductions. "This is Dr. Mukherji, who has agreed to see a few patients. But don't waste her time, make certain first that they are willing to trust in the expert advice of a woman."

"I'm happy to assist in any way I can," Piyali said.

His grandmother's gnarled hands gripped Piyali's. "*A'i hon yw hi?*" she asked. *Is this her?* His *mamgu* had insisted they learn the Welsh language when she came to live with them after diphtheria stole away most of his family. "The woman whose hand ought to wear opals and diamonds?"

Evan cleared his throat, replying in the same language. "Yes. Perhaps. There are complications to resolve first."

His sister's eyes widened.

Piyali turned to him with raised eyebrows. Unfair, using Welsh to speak around her in this manner.

"We have much to talk about, Dr. Mukherji," Megan said, switching the conversation back to English. "The moment word gets out, our shop will be overrun today by people seeking your combined expertise. Evan, did you bring more of that miraculous eczema cream? One child in particular is in desperate need."

"I did. Among other things." He reached into the bed of the wagon and handed her a jar. "Before I tie on an apron and set to work, I need to escort Dr. Mukherji across town. She's in need of a specialized piece of medical equipment that might prove difficult to find."

"Oh, no you don't, Evan," Megan chided as she untied her apron and pressed it into his hands. "The list of items you need to attend to here is longer than my arm. Step to it. I'll take Dr. Mukherji to Colonel Pickering's. If anyone's likely to have medical devices, it'll be him."

His sister would spend the entire trip quizzing Piyali about... well... all things related to that opal ring. He opened his mouth to object, but Megan gave him no choice. She slid her arm through Piyali's and dragged her down the street peppering her with questions.

Though Piyali glanced back at him over her shoulder with pleading eyes, she was a trained Queen's agent. With a pistol on her hip. He had every confidence she would survive the interrogation. Better her than him.

"While we hunt down this aetheroscope attachment piece," Megan said, her arm tight, offering Piyali no illusion of escape as she turned into a delightful shopping arcade, "might we discuss weddings?"

Her stomach dropped. If Evan had mentioned her, that he planned to marry, that conversation lay far in the past. A wedding was not at all a certainty now, though she desperately hoped to one day call Megan her sister.

"You're engaged?" Piyali deflected, as a touch of panic crept its way up into her throat. "Many congratulations! Who is the lucky man?"

"Not me," Megan laughed. "Though I've suitors aplenty, I've yet to find one who makes my heart beat faster." She squeezed Piyali's arm tighter. "Yours. To my brother. He teased us before leaving for Brazil, telling us only that his future bride was an Indian woman born in Calcutta. I've studied the wedding traditions. A red gown—a *sari*—embroidered in gold is traditional, correct? Will you arrive in a *palki*?"

"A sedan chair? Through the streets of London?" Piyali cringed in horror, though she wouldn't put it past Ma to try to arrange such an event. A quick simple ceremony in the front parlor would suit her much better. She looked at Megan's face, so full of excitement, and sighed. Perhaps a small, traditional ceremony. Oh, who was she kidding? Small meant hundreds of people, even if her mother was forced to confine the event to the ballroom of her London townhouse. None of which would happen if she couldn't save Evan. "I'm afraid we've rather a serious obstacle in our path. I can't share the details with you. Suffice it to say we need that aetheroscope objective badly."

"Are you ill?" Megan's eyes widened. "Is Evan?"

"Something like that. I'm sorry. I'm sworn to secrecy." By the Queen's agents, by Evan himself. Pulled in two directions, Piyali had a nagging suspicion her loyalty to both would soon be put to the test. Always, her career was a wedge between them.

She pressed her hand against a Babbage card tucked into a pocket, a card that could send a skeet pigeon winging in the direction of Mr. Black. Guilt weighed heavily upon her, but to send a message so soon would be disloyal to Evan. Three months he'd struggled on his own. She could give him a few more days. Then, if they still had no answers, she would have no choice.

"I'm doing my best to help him. If all goes well..."

For several steps, Megan was silent. "I can't lose my brother. He hates to speak about it, but illness is what carried away our family."

Evan had confided the story to Piyali one dark night as they walked through Hyde Park. Her heart squeezed at the memory of his tale. He'd been fourteen years of age when his father, mother, two brothers and a sister all died within the space of a month. He, Megan and his grandmother alone had survived.

"My family suffered a similar fate. I lost an older sister, a younger brother, and my father to diphtheria as well." *Baba.* She'd been so young—all of five years—that they were no more than a fuzzy memory. Was it better—or worse—to have crystal clear memories of how it had once been? "For a while, it was awful." She remembered Ma's grief. "Then my mother met my stepfather who brought us here. He's given me everything, including two little sisters, and the love of a father."

Megan reached out and squeezed her arm. "I'm sorry."
Piyali gave a tight nod. Their losses were the reason
for both Evan's chosen profession and for her own, for
the drive that pushed them both to seek to cure all
manner of infections. She changed the subject. "How
did you convince Evan to accept the grant to travel to
Brazil? He almost turned the committee down, he was
so worried about leaving you and your grandmother
behind, unprotected."

"Yes, always worried for my future," Megan scoffed.
"How? I threatened, at the age of sixteen, to wed a
man twice my age to ensure my so-called security. As
he did not care much for Mr. Jones, after much heated
discussion, he agreed to leave me with Grandmother."
She rolled her eyes. "For the sake of appearances, a
cousin looked in on us during his time abroad, providing
that all-so-necessary male authority."

They shared a knowing look as they came to a stop
before a shop. Emblazoned across the storefront in gilded
lettering: *Colonel Pickering & Company's Scientific
Gadgetries and Curiosities.* Dusty, dark and dimly lit.
Piyali squinted through a window pane and came face to
face with the stuffed head of a quail sewn onto the neck
of a squirrel. The chimera wore a miniature tiara. Such...
décor did not provide her with much hope for scientific
equipment, at least, not equipment that *functioned.*

"He keeps the legitimate items in the back, away
from sticky fingers," Megan said, reading her mind.

They stepped inside. Useless oddities of all kinds were mounted upon display counters, the better to lure in the gullible. But in the back, boxes upon boxes were stacked from floor to ceiling. Perhaps there was some hope. A man emerged from a back room. "Colonel, we have need of a..."

"Crystalline aetheric objective," Piyali finished.

"Right this way, dearies." The colonel's eyes twinkled behind a mass of grizzled facial hair, and she suspected he grinned at the thought of lightening her pockets by several pounds.

Chapter Six

After a long day of patient consults of ailments ranging from croup to toenail fungus—during which mild suspicion of her origins had been overcome by the promise of pain relief and treatment—Piyali was exhausted and all too happy to climb back onto Evan's crank wagon and head for Aberwyn. This time, he arranged for her to sit between him and Sarah.

Not that such a maneuver stopped the other woman. Setting down a stack of thick, paper-wrapped textbooks, Sarah exclaimed, "Oh, no! My gown!" Her fingers fluttered over a dark smudge upon her bodice, drawing attention to its low-cut neckline. "Mother will have a fit!"

Beside her, Evan sighed. He tugged a handkerchief from his waistcoat and passed it to Piyali. "Here. Save her from her mother's wrath." He kept his eyes carefully focused upon the road before them. "Please."

"It's probably only a touch of dust, most likely from the bookstore," Piyali said, using the square of linen to brush at the smudge, but her efforts only seemed to grind the dirt into the pale, pink fabric. "Um."

"Let me." Sarah snatched the handkerchief from her and made far better progress. "Did you find what you needed?"

"We did," Piyali answered. In a dark, dusty recess of Colonel Pickering's storage room. She'd all but given up hope. Just as they'd been about to try another store, the wizened old man had stumbled—coughing—out from among a pile of dusty boxes holding aloft a small box. Inside, an older model of the objective lay nestled in cotton batting. With luck it would be adequate. She clutched it in her lap now, wrapped and padded against the rigors of traveling over rock-studded roads.

After a few more awkward moments during which Sarah made several unsuccessful attempts to flirt with Evan, Piyali—tired though she was—attempted to buoy her spirits by suggesting a tutoring session. Gleefully, Sarah unwrapped one of her books—a chemistry text— and by the time they arrived at the tavern, they had explored John Dalton's atomic theory, the periodic table of the elements, and the concept of whole-number ratios forming chemical compounds.

"I predict a successful admissions exam," Piyali said, impressed. "You've a sharp mind and will go far."

Sarah drew her shoulders back at the compliment. Had anyone ever praised her for her mind? Given her buxom milkmaid appearance and the bar's clientele, the likely answer was no. "Mother would be furious if she learned of my plans, so tell no one. Better she believes I'm reading penny dreadfuls. You go in first, I'll scurry behind and hide these textbooks away."

Evan, who had been largely silent the entire ride home, spoke. "Dr. Mukherji shall accompany me to my laboratory." He walked about the wagon to offer the young woman a hand down. "We've a bit of a mystery to unravel."

Sarah tipped her head. "As in experimental?" Piyali nodded and Sarah's face grew somber as she hopped from the cart. "I admit, I'd love to see Tegan fall face-down in a mud puddle. But not die from some obscure infection. Is it serious?"

"It is," Piyali said and pressed a finger to her lips. "*Shh.* Not a word to anyone." After moment's hesitation, she added, "Keep an eye on your mother."

Frowning, Evan climbed back onto the cart. He gripped the steering wheel and released the break, setting the crank wagon lumbering along the road. "She's a terrible gossip."

"She guessed," Piyali defended. "And knows nothing about the frog."

They drew up before his stone cottage with its moss-covered slate roof. She barely spared it a glance as she waited for Evan to unlock the door before hurrying to her aetheroscope at his desk. Time was of the essence. A remedy was desperately needed, and, if she could solve this quickly and present a cure, perhaps Mr. Black wouldn't relieve her of her weapon and consign her to her laboratory.

Conscious of the Babbage card she'd elected not to employ, Piyali wasted no time replacing the broken objective. She had a glass slide prepped and ready before she noticed Evan was not at her side. She looked up to find him frowning at the shelves that held jars and boxes of his chemicals and concoctions. "Is something wrong?" she asked.

"Someone has been here in our absence," he stated, gloves clutched tightly in one hand. "The *nah-puh-de-ot* ought to be next to the *o-ko-ne-de-kuh*, in clear alphabetical order. Look," he pointed, "this jar, it's been rotated such that the label is not easily readable."

"Theft?" Piyali had no idea what those plants were, but if he was concerned... "But the cottage is locked." Her forehead wrinkled. She'd seen the advanced lock he'd installed, both on the greenhouse door and the cottage door. "Quite securely." An agent might be able to break it, but it wouldn't be easily cracked by someone in search of free medication.

"So it is." Evan lifted each jar, examining its contents, replacing it upon the shelf. "I've not a clue who would go to such lengths. I've always reduced—or outright refused—payment if a client couldn't afford it." He set down the final jar with a grimace. "The minute a medication proves successful, I provide as much product as the plant's growth will bear."

"Has anything like this, anything unusual, occurred before?"

His brow furrowed.

"What is it?"

"Last week, the night before Tegan was bitten, I found the door to my greenhouse ajar. I installed the lock the next day, but I expect it's how the frog escaped."

"Frog!" Piyali jumped to her feet and ran into the greenhouse, Evan following close behind. The frog still crouched in its terrarium, safe, happy and blue. "Thank goodness." The frog was not involved. She dug for an explanation. "You have a number of projects underway, all experimental. Have you boasted of initial success to anyone in so much as a simple letter?" Piyali went still as her words loomed between them, a specter from their past. She swallowed nervously.

"I'm sorry," Evan said, his gray-blue eyes softening as they focused upon her. "I didn't know what to say... I didn't want to drag you into this disaster, and then I decided it was best if I didn't write at all. I should have replied, I should have said... something. Can you forgive me?"

Could she? All too easily. But if they couldn't solve this... problem, if she reported it to Mr. Black, could he forgive her? "Of course," she whispered.

His hand glimmered with heightened emotion, and he reached for her and caught her hand. Heat shimmered in his eyes. "Come with me, upstairs."

"Not yet." Her entire body—ablaze with heated anticipation—objected to her words, but her brain insisted. "First, I want answers." The question would nag at her until it was answered. She smiled coyly. "Only then can I give you my *full* attention."

"Work before play." He stroked his thumb across her palm, sending a shiver down her spine. "I gather the new objective is installed and ready for use?"

"All I need is a fresh biopsy," she stuttered.

"Then grab your razor." His voice rasped across her skin. "At the moment, there's only one thing I'd like better than a definitive diagnosis."

Minutes later, perched on a chair before the desk, she slid the prepared slide into the aether chamber and screwed in a canister of compressed gas. The seal popped and a low hiss indicated the chamber was filling. Staring through the eyepiece, she first brought his skin biopsy into focus using the lower magnification objectives, finally spinning in the new high-powered lens and carefully adjusting focus.

There lay the answer. But only part of it. She stared, not quite able to believe her vision wasn't playing tricks upon her. This shouldn't be possible, not in a mammalian species.

Evan cleared his throat, then spoke with an unsteady voice. "What is it?"

Piyali lifted her gaze to his. "It's your melanocytes."

He shook his head. "I only know plant histology."

"Your epidermis, the top layer of your skin, is comprised of several layers dominated by keratinocytes—layers upon layers of flattened cells. Tucked among the cells in the basal layer—the deepest layer of the epidermis—are cells known as melanocytes. These are the cells that produce a protein responsible for skin pigmentation called melanin. Normally, the pigment is of a brown or black color."

Understanding dawned on Evan's face. "Are you telling me that my affected skin has blue melanin?"

"Not exactly," she hedged. "It's iridescent, and I wouldn't call the pigment melanin. In any case, that's not what the cells are making, not anymore. They're producing an entirely different substance."

Running a finger beneath his collar, he asked, "Do you know what it is?"

"Yes. I've seen this before, but never in humans. Guanine crystals appear to have replaced your normal pigment."

"Guanine crystals." Confusion creased his brow.

"You've seen the effect before, in fish most likely," she said. "The silvery flash of scales as they swim. More tropical varieties can produce stunning shades of a variety of colors—blues, reds, yellows. It's also common in reptiles and amphibians. Normally, however, the colors are static. In your case, however, the angle of the crystal can change, altering the color of light that is reflected back."

Evan swore and stabbed his fingers into his hair. "I'm a bloody chameleon?"

"Of course not. But your comparison is apt in that you do possess the ability to color shift. Some scientists hypothesize that the flat, plate-like crystals are stacked, one upon another into a kind of lattice that can be actively adjusted."

"Which would explain why the infected members of the tribe, when angry or upset or afraid, would *disappear* into the rainforest." He threw a hand in the air and began to pace. "They were simply mirroring all the colors around them."

"I expect so." Her mouth tugged into a frown. How to break it to him?

"I don't like your expression, Piyali." He closed his eyes for a brief moment. "I'm not going to like this, am I? Maybe I should just look."

"Wait." She put her hand over the eyepiece. "There's good news and bad news." Evan groaned. "I've found the organism responsible. You have an intracellular parasite. It's not transmissible because it's creeping along beneath your skin at the basal layer."

"A parasite?" He grimaced, rubbing his shimmering hand. "Please tell me that's the bad news."

"I'm afraid not," she said. "The bad news is that I've never seen—or heard—of anything like it. But now that we can *see* it, we'll be able to quickly determine if any of the chemicals and drugs are taking effect."

"Let me see if I have this straight." He pinched the bridge of his nose. "An intracellular parasite entered my skin via a frog's bite. This tiny creature worked its way into my melanocytes, somehow altering the chemical makeup of my melanin—or replacing it, turning it blue."

It was more than simple replacement, but the description was apt. "Unless you're affected by strong emotion as you are now," she reminded him, recalling the first time she'd seen his hand color shift. It was the moment she'd realized there was still hope for them.

"At which point I shimmer pink and silver like a soap bubble." His lips twisted and his voice was wry. "How very lovely. If we manage to kill this parasite—"

Reaching out, she placed her hand on his arm. There was nothing she wouldn't do to solve this, to find a way to stop this parasite. "We will."

He raised an eyebrow in doubt. "If. Will my skin return to its normal color?"

"I don't know," she admitted. "Perhaps, if the presence of a living parasite is necessary to provide the melanocyte with whatever code is necessary to produce guanine crystals... or it might be permanent. Either way, if we stop it now—"

"At least my face won't turn blue."

As long as he was hers, Piyali didn't much care what color his skin turned. Not that such a declaration would bring him any relief. If brown skin placed one on the edge of respectability, blue skin... Well, who wanted to be treated like a carnival side show?

When Evan finally peered through the eyepiece of Piyali's aetheroscope, he could hardly believe that such small, cigar-shaped creatures were the cause of all his problems. The biopsied melanocytes collected from his hand contained but one or two parasites, but those cells collected closer to his shoulder—where the infestation continued to spread toward his neck—were teaming with the creatures, all creeping toward the front edge poised for migration.

He imagined them crying out, "Onward and upward!" It seemed the only thing slowing them down was the ointment he'd concocted. Some component of that compound contained toxins. If they could isolate it, then concentrate it, perhaps there was a chance of ending—if not completely reversing—this nightmare.

Only then could she again be his.

Grabbing a machete, he stalked into the greenhouse to cut down one of the many *khu-neh-ari* lianas tangling through overhead branches.

"Evan," she said quietly, following him. He could tell from her voice that she was about to broach an uncomfortable topic. "I know you wish to keep this secret—and why. I've not contacted Mr. Black, but if we can't devise a cure and soon, I'll need to let him know. With all of Lister University's resources, with all their chemists working on this, progress will be fast."

She wanted him cured. Given how his heart ached at the thought of a life without her, he understood. Not enough, however, to place a powerful, infectious biological agent into the hands of the government. It would be misused. Of that he was certain.

"A few days," he hedged, slicing through the fibrous vines of the climbing shrub, a liana, and handing her a segment. With luck, perhaps they could avoid this argument. "This is the *khu-neh-ari* plant, the one I used to make the ointment."

As she studied the leafy vine in her hand, lines of worry carved themselves between her eyebrows. "How do we go about this?" she asked. "Sorting one component from another."

"Chromatography. Extraction and isolation of components. Distillation. Testing—over and over and over until we find the right dose, the right combination." He cut free another branch and handed it to her. "I was taught to boil the leaves for two days, adding a handful of large stinging ants. I have a limited supply of those in dried form."

Piyali gagged. "Along with eye of newt and wing of bat?"

He grinned. "The ointment works, doesn't it?"

"Not quite well enough." A determined look was back in her eyes. Cure him she would.

God, I hope so.

A glimmer of moonlight fell upon her cheek. Instead of reaching for another branch, he stroked her skin, that silky, smooth slope, with the back of his finger. "I never stopped loving you, Piyali, not once. Every night I would climb into my hammock beneath swaths of mosquito netting and think of nothing but returning to you."

Pressing his hand against her face, she looked up into his eyes with such sadness. "Then why hide this from me?"

"I didn't know if it was contagious. I didn't know how fast it would spread, how quickly it would consume me. Like me, you watched your own family die, one person at a time. I didn't want you to have to endure that again, watching a loved one die, unable to do anything." It was why he'd tossed his reply to her into the fire, abandoning all hope of a wife and family. "It was hell."

"But you wouldn't have wanted to be anywhere but at their side. When you didn't answer, when the skeet pigeon didn't return, I thought…" A tear slid from the corner of her eye and Evan's heart almost broke, and his lungs felt heavy, as if they might fail to inflate. "I thought you'd realized I was a mistake, that you'd come home to find a Welsh girl from your childhood had grown into the woman of your dreams."

"Never." He threw aside the machete and brought his other hand to her face. "You are everything to me. I thought it better if I simply disappeared from your life." His thumb brushed aside a new tear. "You have so much potential, so much talent, hiding here—with me—in the forests of Wales would be the world's loss. I was so proud when I heard you'd won a laboratory of your own at Lister University." He smiled. "And now you're a Queen's agent with a pistol on your hip... it makes you irresistible."

An answering smile tugged at her rosy, full lips. "Irresistible?"

The experiments could wait. Evan pulled the cut branches from her hands and tossed them in the general direction of the cottage door. He hauled her up against his chest and kissed her exactly as he'd dreamed about doing all those nights alone in the rainforest. She tasted soft and sweet—of everything that meant home.

Moaning, Piyali parted her lips and ran her hands over the linen of his shirt, making appreciative sounds as she explored the shape of his muscles. As his tongue delved deeper their kiss grew hungrier, touching a match to dry tinder.

Heat shot down his spine, gathering low. Kissing her wasn't enough. He needed her silky, bare skin sliding against his own, and there would be no focusing on anything else until such primal demands were metHe dragged his mouth from hers. "Not here."

"Why not? The cloakroom didn't stop you." Her voice held a breathless note, as her fingertip traced the blue tendrils that radiated from his shoulder across his chest and about his neck. "You've no need to hide anything from me."

Even at his most vulnerable, laid bare before her eyes, she made him feel whole. Scooping her into his arms, he carried her back into the cottage and up the stairs. "Those walls weren't glass, and this time I want to see everything."

CHAPTER SEVEN

*E*verything.

Nervous embarrassment hovered in her eyes, but she was no innocent. Their encounter in the Pharmacological Society's shadowy cloakroom—their joining desperate and frantic and wonderful—had seen to that. He'd clung to that memory, a memory he'd unsuccessfully tried to cram into a dark corner of his heart and lock away. His groin throbbed with need, but as much as he wanted to be inside her again, this time he wanted to *see* her.

He set her down on the edge of his bed and knelt before her to unlace her knee-high leather boots, but the way she bit her lower lip made his fingers pause as conflict gripped him. "I can only promise you today. If that's not enough, we'll stop." Though he might explode with the effort.

"I'm not asking you for forever." Piyali threaded her fingers through his curls and tipped his face upward. "Don't stop. Even if everything falls apart, I want this. Here. Now."

"Good. Because I don't think I can manage to wait much longer." He yanked the boots from her feet and threw them aside. His own shoes joined them. Without bothering to fully unbutton his shirt, he dragged it over his head. She shifted to unbuckle her corset, then, unclasping hooks, she slid her *choli* down her arms, leaving herself bare to the waist.

He let out a low whistle. "I knew I was missing out last time. So beautiful," he murmured, sweeping his palm over her breast as her nipples puckered under his gaze, "and begging for attention." Dipping his head, he caught the tight bud between his lips and sucked. With a moan, she gripped his head, holding him close.

Her back arched. "Oh, Evan!"

Cries of pleasure that had haunted his dreams fell from her lips, and he lapped in each one even as an unwanted thought crept into his mind. She was not his to keep. Not yet. Perhaps never. This explosion of longing, these shared moments of intimacy might be their last. All the more reason to treasure every one. Inhaling her sweet scent, he sent his hands wandering over the dips and curves of her body.

Hands. Hers were on his shoulders now, sliding over his biceps, then gripping his muscles. With the edge of his teeth, he scraped the tip of her nipple and was rewarded with a tight gasp—and the sharp bite of her nails into his skin. A heartbeat later and her fingers trailed over his chest, landing on the top button of his trousers, loosening it. He wanted this to last, but it wouldn't. Not if she wrapped her hands around his hard length. With a gentle push, he sent her falling backward onto the thick, down-filled mattress.

"You first." Bending over, he slid his hands over her soft skin, catching at the drawstring of her *lehenga*. A quick tug with his fingers, and the garment loosened. With a gentle kiss to her navel, he whisked away the satiny garment and lay her bare to his view. But before he could return his mouth to her skin, she rolled onto her side, propping herself on one elbow. Her long braid fell over her shoulder, and she toyed with its end, unfastening the tie that held the plaits in place.

"Take them off," she said, her eyes slightly unfocused. "You're not the only one who wants to look." She ran her fingers through her hair, freeing its long, silky lengths. "Take them off and join me."

All too happy to oblige, he yanked his trousers off and climbed onto the bed, stretching out beside her and skimming his hand over the curve of her hip. "So soft."

"So long," she said, her voice sultry as she traced his length. He clenched his jaw, wanting her touch but desperately trying to maintain control. His member throbbed as her slender fingers wrapped about him. "So thick and hard." Her flashing eyes teased. "Remind me how we fit together, for it doesn't seem possible."

"No?" He caught her wrist. Much more of that and he wouldn't last long enough to slide inside her. Encircling both wrists with one hand, he rolled her onto her back—then lifted her arms above her head, thrusting her gorgeous breasts upward. "Let me remind you." He brushed a finger across the soft curls at the apex of her thighs, then slipped a fingertip along the seam of her wet heat. Her well-kissed lips parted and her breath came faster as he circled her center. "Remembering now?"

Eyes closed, her dark lashes fanned across her cheeks. "A glimmer," she breathed, tipping her hips and parting her knees. "But I recall a bit more *depth* to your explorations."

Nipping the delicate skin of her neck, he laughed against her skin, then slid a finger deep inside her hot, wet channel. "Like this?" he asked, pushing slowly in and out of her. He watched, greedy for the vision of her pleasure. Their first time together had been one of touch and taste—he'd missed the sight of her hips flexing against his hand, her back arching, her heels digging into the mattress.

"More," she gasped. "All of you, Evan. Fill me."

In no frame of mind to deny such a plea, he rolled, dragging her with him, across him, crushing her heavy breasts to his chest. Her hips to his. Needing to be inside her, he guided her leg over his hip.

"You want me... on top?" She rose up onto her knees, straddling him, lowering herself onto his throbbing member. Long, dark hair fanned about her face and over her shoulders, its ends a gentle tease against his hot skin. His breath caught as she flexed her hips, gliding her wetness over his arousal. "Like this?"

He groaned, and his answer was strangled, but he managed a retort. "Exactly that way, but with more depth." It was her turn to laugh as he reached for a paper package upon his bedside table and pressed the sheath into her hand. No good pharmacist should be without one. He'd snatched a box at the store, hoping... "Cover me, then take me inside you."

Sweet torture, her soft hands moving over his stiff rod. He dug his fingers into the sheets, fighting a need to surge upward. At last, she notched him against her opening and took a few inches of him inside. Slowly, she pulled away before easing him back into tightness and wet heat.

"Oh, yes," she said, spreading her thighs wider, sinking onto him and finally, finally, finally taking him fully within her. "This is the delicious fullness I remember," she said, her voice a low purr.

With a growl, he jerked his hips upward. "There's more moving involved."

"Is there?" she teased, holding perfectly and painfully still. She leaned forward onto her hands and took his lips with hers. A deep, soul-shattering kiss. He let go of the bed and pulled her face to his. As they kissed, her hips began to move, slowly at first, rising and falling upon his length until he tore his mouth away on a groan.

Reaching between them, he pressed a thumb to her swollen bud, and her hips bucked, taking him deeper. "Yes!" She threw her head back. Waves of hair tumbled over her shoulders as her back arched, tipping her breasts upward. Piyali, wild and beautiful. An image he'd never forget. "Oh, God, Evan. Don't stop."

His body tightened, tension coiling at the base of his spine, but he held back, wanting to wait until she found her pleasure. He clenched his jaw, trying to hold on, but he wasn't going to last much longer. She was so perfect and it had been so long. Too long. He gripped her hips, his fingers digging into the soft flesh of her buttocks, and buried himself in her.

"Yes!" she cried.

Her hips jerked against his, and her sheath clenched about his shaft while her face contorted with pleasure. At last, he let himself go, diving deep to bury himself within her. His climax tore through him, his heart pounding wildly as he plummeted over the edge.

She collapsed onto his chest, her hair falling about them like a curtain, shutting out the world so that only the two of them were left. He wrapped his arms about her waist, holding her tight as their ragged breaths slowly returned to normal.

"I love you so much, Piyali," he whispered, brushing a strand of hair from her face. Long ago he'd professed his love, and he'd not hold it back from her now. Not when it was the only thing he could give. He couldn't promise her forever, not yet, but she should know that she would always have his heart.

She loved him too. But the words wouldn't pass her lips. Suppressed anger that he'd not called upon her for help the moment he'd known something was wrong? Or the nagging feeling of disloyalty to the Crown? It was a most uncomfortable position. She ought to report her findings concerning the origins of the blue lesion. But to do so was to betray Evan's confidence.

Or was it simply that she could only offer such words to someone who promised her forever, no matter how short forever was? A promise he would not make. Not yet.

Lying here curled in his arms, body and emotions laid bare, she couldn't bring herself to speak, to destroy the illusion that all was well. But even now, even as his glimmering fingers traced a slow, seductive path over the dip of her waist, the curve of her hip, her mind puzzled over how the infection might—at the very least—be stopped in its tracks. For it had to be stopped. This intracellular parasite could not be allowed to steal away her heart's desire.

"We need to get back to work," she said, breaking the silence. She rolled away, reaching for her discarded *lehenga choli*. "At some point, Mr. Black will take note of my failure to report." While she was willing to delay that particular missive, she would not compose an outright lie.

Evan groaned, but he too pried himself from the mattress and stood, discarding the sheath. "The minute we solve this problem, I'm dragging you back to bed— and we're staying there. For hours, if not days."

Glancing over her shoulder, she treated herself to one last glimpse of his toe-curling physique. Her heart leapt at the dark and sultry look he cast in her direction, a contemplation of all manner of erotic activities. The muscles of his broad shoulders, of his defined pectoral muscles shifted as he tugged on his shirt. Tempting, to reach out with her fingertips and trace the ridges of his stomach that marched downward toward a resurging interest in bedroom activities.

"Then let's begin." After dressing, she padded down the stairs and crossed to the iron stove, adding a block of peat to the fire and setting a pot of water onto the range. "Boiling leaves and dried ants. Primitive. My mentors would recoil in shock and horror." But not her *dida*. How many times had Piyali watched her grandmother boil *methi*—fenugreek—to make tea for settling her stomach and balancing her blood? Though in this particular case, *dida's* bottle of neem oil might prove more useful as an anti-parasitic.

"Back to the basics, with refinement to follow." Evan's voice rumbled over her skin, a sensual distraction she forced herself to ignore—until he caught her in his arms for one last kiss, leaving her breathless, her determination to resist his charms cracking and crumbling. "I'll gather the *khu-neh-ari* branches," he said, then took himself off to the greenhouse.

Fanning her hot face with her hand, Piyali examined the shelves of his supplies, contemplating a variety of options. Pharmacology was not her specialty, but she knew the basics, and so—braiding her hair and knotting a string about its end—began to gather any and all supplies that held even the faintest promise of a cure. Bottles and jars accumulated: black drawing salve, boric acid, calamine, castor oil, chaulmoogra oil, copper sulfate, gentian violet, iodine, mercurous chloride, sulfur, turpentine...

Hours later, glass Petri dishes covered the table's surface. Each held a small sample of biopsies of Evan's blue skin to which a variety of treatments—botanical and chemical—had been applied. Including the leaf and ant concoction. Conditions weren't perfect, but it was the best they could do without a fully outfitted laboratory. The heat of the stove would keep the cultures warm, if not exactly at body temperature. Piyali clung to the hope that one of their makeshift experiments would yield results.

Now they waited.

"Evan," she said, slipping behind him to wrap her arms about his waist and press the side of her face to his broad back. She choked out words her heart advised against. "It's nearly midnight. I need to go back to the tavern." By now Sarah—and the entire village—would have taken note of her failure to return, and she did not wish to antagonize them.

"Stay." He wrapped a strong hand around hers.

"I shouldn't. You know as well as I that gossip will be bubbling. If you want to conceal our relationship, that isn't the way of going about it." Agreeing to the here and now hurt, but if it was all they'd ever have, she would grab it with both hands. However, there was his sister to consider. Though she hesitated to broach the topic, she forced the words past her lips. "Without a wedding on the horizon, gossip will wend its way to Cardiff and impact Megan's future."

He sighed, but nodded. "I'll walk you back."

Ignoring the ache in her heart, Piyali lifted her bag and followed Evan out onto the moonlit path that wended its way down the hillside. Halfway, a flickering glow illuminated the forest glen and the fairy well it cradled.

Swearing beneath his breath, Evan came to a sudden stop. His arm looped about her as she stumbled into his solid form.

"What is it?" she whispered into his ear.

"It's Seren's Day." He turned her around. "We'll need to take a different path."

"Wait." Curiosity pricked, and she stepped past him, creeping closer to the well, taking care to stay well-hidden behind a nearby tree.

A number of young women—including Sarah and Tegan—gathered in a circle about the pool of water, looking remarkably serious. Each held a flickering candle in their left hand and pinched something between their right forefinger and thumb. With a glint of silver, one girl tossed her offering into the well, murmuring something— Welsh from the sound of it—and peered into the moonlit pool. There was a collective inhale, a holding of breaths, then a giggle, a blush and the announcement of a name. "Aled."

"What on earth are they doing?" Piyali whispered as the next woman stepped forward. A time-honored ritual, but to what end?

"Tonight's the night when a maiden can toss a bent pin into the well to ask the *gwragedd annwn* to show them the face of their future husband."

"*Gwragedd annwn*?" Piyali tried to wrap her tongue around the strange Welsh words and failed.

"The water-sprite, a kind of fairy, that lives in this well. A few would even have you believe that a woman can—with the right words and offerings—coax the water-sprite into delivering the man of her choice into her arms." He scoffed. "Sheer nonsense."

"They seem quite serious," Piyali observed, intrigued by the age-old custom and the seriousness of the ceremony.

"Mmm," Evan answered.

Sarah's turn arrived. She mouthed the words, tossed the pin, but instead of bending over to look, tossed in a scrap of cloth.

"That's cheating!" Tegan accused, rounding on her. The harsh tone of her voice shattered the sacred silence. "You stole that handkerchief from him."

Him. *Evan's* missing handkerchief.

Smirking, Sarah gave a half shrug. "*You* snuck up here days ago, trying to coax the *gwragedd annwn* to do your bidding. *That* is cheating. At least I'm open about my wishes."

"I did not!" Tegan pointed a finger. "You sent your mother to appeal to the sprite on your behalf."

There was a collective gasp from the group of women. "Shh," one admonished. "You'll frighten the *gwragedd annwn* away."

"At least I'm not creeping about Evan's greenhouse," Sarah said, "peering in windows or throwing myself at him with any number of ridiculous and fictitious afflictions. I hope your entire leg turns blue and falls off."

With a howl, Tegan launched herself at Sarah, grabbing her by the hair and dragging them both into the shallow water. Both of them screamed, clawing at each other with their fingers, splashing and thrashing, each trying to hold the other's face beneath the water.

"Stop!" The women cried out, leaping away from the brawl. A few—those who had yet to make their appeal to the water-sprite—burst into tears.

"That's enough!" Evan bellowed as he stepped from behind the tree. "Stop this nonsense immediately. Home, all of you." There was a slight hesitation as horrified faces turned in his direction, and then the women began to move, running down the pathway. He reached over the low stone wall and hauled Tegan away from Sarah.

"Ow!" Sarah cried as she crawled to the muddy edge of the pool, clutching at her lower leg. "I think it's broken!"

"Now who exaggerates!" Tegan yelled.

"That's enough!" he barked, scooping Sarah into his arms and leaving a sour-faced Tegan sitting half-submerged in the pool. "Once you manage to control your temper, Piyali will assist you."

Reluctantly, Piyali extended a hand, but Tegan only narrowed her eyes. Several long gashes reddened where fingernails had streaked down her face. "You," she spat. "You've ruined everything." Thrashing about, the young woman dragged herself from the pool, and set off down the path behind Evan.

CHAPTER EIGHT

Evan kicked the tavern door open and stepped into its smoky, alcohol-steeped interior. A number of men whooped to see him carrying Miss Sarah Parker, her arms wrapped tightly about his neck and her face pressed to his chest. Picking her up was a mistake he'd immediately regretted, but what was the alternative?

"What are you doing with my daughter?" Mr. Parker barked. "That's it, I'm calling the—"

"I'm *not* marrying her." A statement he made *every* time he walked through this door of late. He plopped Sarah's sodden form down on the nearest chair and pried her arms from his neck. Her torn bodice gaped. "Dr. Mukherji and I found her—and others—at Seren's Well. Miss Price and Miss Parker had an... altercation. Miss Parker has injured her ankle."

This announcement drew forth another round of whoops, including table slapping along with a number of ribald comments and speculation as to who had won the catfight. Congratulations were called out to Sarah, who wore a satisfied smile at all the attention.

"What happened to Tegan?" he asked Piyali softly.

"She refused my hand," she muttered. "And called you a number of creative names as she stumbled home."

He cringed. "I'm sorry, but we shall have to pay her a visit later." It was the last thing she wished do, but it was the *right* thing to do.

She jerked a nod. "Let me see to Sarah's leg first."

Dragging up her wet skirts, a whimper escaped Sarah's mouth. "There's a reason we call her two-faced Tegan." A deep, bloody gash cut through her stocking and into the skin of her calf.

Piyali set down her bag and bent to examine the wound. "That's going to require stitches." Painful ones. "Where is your mother? You should change into clean, dry clothes before I employ my suture kit."

"She's not available," Mr. Parker said, placing a hand on his daughter's shoulder, pressing her into the chair. "Stay." He nodded at Piyali. "Much obliged if you'd sew her back together."

"Your wife, is she ill?" Evan asked, recalling the accusation Tegan had hurled at Sarah—and Piyali's report that Mrs. Parker had also been bitten by the blue frog. Much as he disliked the woman, he couldn't ignore the possibility that she too might have need of treatment. His initial "rash" had spread all too fast. "I've heard reports that she's favoring a hand. Shall I take a look at her injury?"

"She's fine." Mr. Parker's words were gruff, leaving no doubt in Evan's mind that he would never, ever, under any circumstances be allowed to attend his wife. His daughter's injury, however, couldn't be dismissed.

After much drama involving screams and tears and shots of gin to calm a much-distressed patient, Mr. Parker carried his now-contrite, inebriated daughter to her room.

A heavy sigh met his ears as Piyali followed him out of the tavern. It was well past midnight. "Tegan?" she asked. Her hand sought his, and he grasped it tightly, squeezing. A small comfort. But it wasn't enough.

"Her injuries were minor," he answered. "Better to call upon her in the morning." With a tug, he pulled Piyali into his arms and out of sight of the tavern's dirt-streaked windows. He slanted his mouth over hers and kissed her until she melted against him, until he nearly threw propriety to the wind and hauled her back to his cottage. Gossip be damned. Reluctantly, he released her. "Go. Sleep. We've much to do tomorrow. Today."

"We do." She lifted a hand to drag her palm across the stubble on his cheek. "I've missed you so much, Evan. We will solve this..."

The silver embroidery upon the hem of her skirt glinted in the moonlight as she stepped back into the tavern. She'd left a few words unspoken, but he'd read her unspoken thought in her eyes, and they sent a shaft of pain deep into his chest.

Whatever the cost.

The cost might very well be calculated by Queen's agents and the scientists who kept Britain's security at the forefront of their minds. Even Piyali struggled to rank him above her loyalty to the Crown. He'd know the minute she tossed a skeet pigeon toward London; guilt would scrawl itself across her face as if written in red ink, for she'd be unable to hide such a decision from him. At which point Tegan's lesion would be excised, and he—and the frog—would disappear from Wales and from her life. Forever. He desperately hoped it wouldn't come to that.

Long before the first rays of sun lightened the sky, Piyali tapped softly at the door to Sarah's chamber. Something about the young woman's wound nagged at the back of her mind. Only examining it, studying its ragged edges and finding nothing abnormal would put her at ease.

The door cracked open and a pair of sleepy eyes set in a drawn face peered out.

"May I come in?" Piyali asked. "I want to make certain there's no infection." Of *any* kind.

Sarah waved her in, dropping back onto her bed and stretching out her leg. "It hurts, but only a little."

"Was it worth it?" she asked as she unwrapped the gauze.

"Even if Evan wants nothing more to do with me, he's at least met the real Tegan. Such a brat." Satisfaction stretched Sarah's lips wide.

Agreeing with her mildly vindictive patient seemed unwise, even if Piyali's heart hummed a happy tune at Evan's inability to resist her charms. For years he'd waited. For her.

"No sign of excessive redness," she said. But neither had Tegan's ankle shown any normal signs of infection. That stray thought had her reaching for the torch at her waist. Not possible. Was it? Better to know than to leave any lingering doubt. Shaking the decilamp, she pointed the beam of light toward Sarah's calf.

A glimmer, a flash and a nightmare unfolded. The edges of the wound—a tiny fraction of an inch—were iridescent. Guanine crystals.

An iron band tightened about her chest; air scraped its way in and out of her lungs. This was a disaster. With the frog in captivity, it could mean only one thing. Whatever parasitic organism lived in the amphibian's salvia, it did not require its host to survive. Despite its tropical origins, the parasite had managed to colonize the cold waters of Seren's Well, entering Sarah's skin via the open wound.

Tegan.

Piyali's stomach clenched. Sarah had dragged four fingernails—four *wet* fingernails—down the side of

Tegan's face. *Her face.* "Keep it clean and rest today," she said, careful to keep her voice steady as she wrapped the wound once again. "I'll have Mr. Tredegar prepare a salve. Be certain to use it."

Outside Sarah's room, Piyali fell against the closed door, pressing a hand to her chest. Her heart pounded against her ribs. What to do? Stepping back into the common room of the tavern, she searched out the rusty skeet pigeon, perched once again upon its shelf, returned from its last delivery. Hers. Odd that Mr. Black had sent no reply. He must still be in Scotland, her message languishing among his extensive correspondence. Not that her note mattered. More than an objective was broken now. An entire well was contaminated, one frequented by the local population. Disaster loomed.

She could delay one more day. If the experiments didn't provide a cure within the next twenty-four hours, she'd have no choice but to write to the head of the Queen's agents, the Duke of Avesbury himself.

This was a complete catastrophe.

Evan stared at the four blue streaks that raked down Tegan's face. Tears ran from her eyes as she blew her red, puffy nose. "I'm going to die!" she keened.

As always, Tegan was completely self-centered. She offered not a single word of apology for instigating the fight, nor showed any concern for how Sarah might have fared. *Sarah.* He ran a hand over his eyes. If Tegan's scratches were so affected, what of Sarah's wound?

Her mother stood beside her, wringing her hands, looking to him with pleading eyes, but all he had to offer her were false promises and an imperfect ointment. Tegan might not die, but the quality of her life was definitely on a downward spiral unless he and Piyali found a cure and soon.

In the doorway, Mr. Price cleared his throat. "Dr. Mukherji has arrived."

Mouth open, Piyali stepped into the room, yet her expression wasn't one of surprise, rather one of horror at the verification of her worst fears.

A ball of lead dropped into his stomach. "Sarah?"

A grim nod was her answer.

There was nothing more they could do here; their time was best spent searching for a cure. Mouthing useless words of encouragement and instructing Mrs. Price to continue to apply the ointment, he grabbed Piyali by the elbow and steered her toward the shop's door. "We'll be back to check on her tonight."

Piyali shook her elbow free. "If I might purchase a jar, Mr. Price?"

"A canning jar?" Mr. Price's voice was incredulous.

"Yes." She dropped a coin into his hand as he handed her the glass container. "Thank you. It'll do."

Evan kept his lips pressed tightly together until they had traveled several feet down the rutted road, exiting the village. "It's not the frog this time."

"No," Piyali agreed. "It's not."

"The experiments are a failure." Ice slid through his veins as he presented a cold and bleak report. "As you predicted, without proper incubation the cultured skin cells died. Even more worrisome, I examined a drop of the culture media beneath the lens of your aetheroscope and," he took a deep breath, "the parasites broke free from the dying cells and are now free-swimming."

Pain, not surprise, crossed her face as she lifted the jar. "In the water of Seren's Well too. It appears they require a wound, a laceration of the epidermis for direct access to the basal layer. Sarah's fingernails digging scratches into Tegan's face. The sharp edge of a stone wall cutting Sarah's ankle." She dragged in a ragged breath. "Evan, I need to write to Mr. Black. The water is contaminated. If anyone seeks the well's healing waters, anyone with so much as a tiny scratch, they too might become infected."

An entire town slipping into madness. There would be no hiding such a crisis. No longer could this be kept a secret. They turned off the main road, following the narrow path upward into the forest, winding their way toward the fairy well. Soon the small, sleepy town of Aberwyn would be overrun with agents of the Crown.

He, Tegan, Sarah—and quite probably her mother— would be quarantined, his sister and grandmother notified. He cringed. For the mental and physical safety of them all, separate—locked—cells would be required. Once the government realized the potential powers behind the side-effects of a blue frog's bite... No, he could not allow himself to contemplate such a bleak future. Not yet.

"One more day," he pleaded, stopping before Seren's Well. Its once innocent waters now teamed with tropical parasites that had colonized an entirely new habitat. "One more day to find a cure."

From the slight sag of his shoulders, Piyali knew it would cost him much to relinquish control. Though it was time to summon assistance, neither was she ready to admit defeat. A small concession was in order. "We'll sample the water," she said. "Confirm our suspicions. We'll set up another round of experiments, and then I'll compose a report. Maybe the parasites will prove easier to kill outside a host."

She lifted a stick from the ground, threading it through the wire handle of the canning jar, and dipped it into the water. Sample collected, she stepped back onto the path, careful to hold the vessel steadily before her.

"Let's hope so," Evan said, his jaw set with determination.

Once the Queen's agents became involved, quarantine was a strong possibility, and they might well judge the situation a security risk, refusing to inform his family of any specifics regarding his health or whereabouts. "If it comes to it, I'll see to your sister and grandmother." Whatever it took.

He managed a stiff nod.

They returned to his cottage in painful silence, neither one of them wishing to speculate as to what the future held.

Soon she was perched once again upon the chair at Evan's desk and bent over to peer through the eyepiece of the aetheroscope. Her skin crawled. Wriggling in the water droplet on the glass slide were hundreds of microscopic organisms.

Evan took one glance and cringed. "Perhaps we ought to consider a more toxic approach, with the primary intent of cleansing the well."

"Chemicals?" she said. "Sodium hypochlorite would bleach the well. It might work, but it will also kill anything else living there. And once the bleach breaks down..." She shook her head. "The well would need to be monitored on a long-term basis. We don't know the life-cycle of this parasite. If it forms a cyst—a tough, protective capsule—in response to environmental insult, it could return the moment conditions are once again favorable."

"We would need to go back to Cardiff to obtain sufficient quantities of bleach to begin treatment. I've only enough here to destroy these samples. As to the problem of potential cysts..." He ran a hand through his hair. "We could post warning signs at the well, inform the entire village, but it won't stop a determined individual from sneaking there in the dark of night and making offerings to the *gwragedd annwn*."

Reaching out, she took Evan's glimmering hand. Frustration had shifted the guanine crystals. She squeezed. "We proceed as planned." She lifted her gaze to his tight eyes and pulled her shoulders back. "Now is not the time to concede defeat, but to redouble our efforts. You were up all night. What components did you manage to extract from the *khu-neh-ari* plant?"

"You're right, of course." Evan drew himself straight. "I've evidence of naphthoquinone..."

They gathered together another collection of plant extracts, chemicals and organic compounds. She reviewed each Petri dish, each test they'd assembled the night before, hoping to find something they'd overlooked.

She didn't.

Piyali set up a dilution series, testing the effectiveness of the few extremely toxic chemicals Evan kept on hand. At last, weary from work and the previous night's events, there was little to do but stare at each other across the table, across a wide selection of Petri dishes, containing well water and a new range of potential anti-parasitic pharmaceuticals. With luck, a few hours from now re-examination would reveal a solution, a chemical and its necessary concentration to eliminate any and all life stages of the parasite. But neither their diligence nor their patience was rewarded. Bleach killed off the parasite, but only when used in unusually large quantities.

"Scrofula!" She slapped her forehead and jumped to her feet. Lack of sleep had fogged her mind. "Sarah! She has no ointment. And, really, I must see if there's a way to convince her mother to allow me to view the bite to her hand."

Evan handed her a small container of his ointment. "She needs to apply it four times a day."

He kissed her forehead, and she wanted nothing more than to wrap her arms about his waist, lay her head on his chest, close her eyes and listen to the steady beat of his heart. Instead, she rose on to the tips of her toes and gave him an all-too-brief kiss. "I'll be back soon," she promised.

CHAPTER NINE

Back at The White Hare, Piyali found Sarah up and about, hoisting trays laden with stew and ale. She tsked. "Eleven stiches warrant a day off."

"Father says there's no place for loafers in our family." Her eyes lifted to the blackened overhead beams of the ceiling, and her next words were louder. "Not that I've seen hide or hair of Mother since I was gravely injured doing *her* bidding."

"*Her* bidding?" Piyali tipped her head.

"I told you the first night you were here." Sarah swatted a hand in the air. "They want me to marry Evan. They've been plaguing and pestering and nudging me in his direction ever since he returned from Brazil." She wiped down a table. "Handsome as he is, wealthy though he might one day be, not once has he offered me any encouragement. Still, I dutifully stole his handkerchief as instructed and tossed a bent pin in a pool of water, mangling some ancient Welsh blessing. And what happens? Tegan, mad as a hatter, drags me into the water, and I end the night with you sewing my leg back together."

"How is your leg?"

"Crusty and sore, if in a sparkling sapphire kind of way." Sarah tipped her head and lifted an eyebrow. "You could have told me. I'm not the type to faint or fret. I do, however, expect you and Evan to provide a cure."

No one could sum up a situation quite like Sarah. With a bitter laugh, she handed Sarah the ointment and gave her instructions. "Your mother ought to use the ointment as well."

"It'll hardly be enough," Sarah said, pulling a face as she slipped the jar into her pocket. "It's spread clear up her arm now. I told her to let you look at it. But no—"

"Sarah!" Mr. Parker yelled from behind the bar. His lips were a harsh, bloodless line and his eyebrows formed a sharply pointed V. "Hush your mouth. I've raised you better than to gossip about family."

Sarah opened her mouth, thought twice, and snapped it shut. Piyali touched her elbow in silent sympathy. With a sidelong glance that spoke of the trials she endured beneath the thumb of her father, Sarah hefted a stack of dirty dishes and wound her way through the tables and chairs to the kitchen.

Curious that Mrs. Parker pushed the centuries old Welsh custom upon her daughter. Wanting Sarah to marry well was understandable, but Piyali wouldn't have pegged Mrs. Parker as the superstitious type.

Now was clearly not the time to press for a visit with Sarah's mother, so Piyali made her way to her room. She'd compose that letter to Mr. Black, then approach Mr. Parker about sending another message. Perhaps that would be the best time to inquire after his wife.

In her room, she placed pen to paper, then stopped. *A frog attack?* Her account read like a fairy tale gone horribly wrong. There had to be a better way to relate the odd events that had occurred in Aberwyn. She scratched out her words and tried again. And again. Tossing aside her fountain pen, Piyali fell backward upon the lumpy mattress. Describing the process by which the man she loved was slowly turning invisible simply was not possible in the small square of parchment a skeet pigeon could carry. Her mind was too muddled. She'd rest her eyes a few minutes, then make another attempt.

The sun was low on the horizon when she pried her eyes open. *Schistosomiasis!* She'd slept away the afternoon. No more time to dally, the evening rush would soon be upon the tavern, and Mr. Parker would only grow more taciturn and gruff without the aid of his wife.

Hastily scratching off a report to Mr. Black containing nothing but bare facts—and trying not to reflect upon how ridiculous it all sounded—she rolled the note into a narrow cylinder, slid it into a tin casing and sealed the end. She bent over her trunk, hunting for another skeet pigeon punch card.

Gone. They were all gone. Her hands stilled as she scanned her belongings. Nothing seemed out of place, and the trunk had been locked. Though, admittedly, her lock was not particularly secure, a mild deterrent. Someone wanted to keep her from contacting headquarters. But who?

Only one person knew she possessed such punch cards. He also happened to be the proprietor of this tavern and inn. Was it Mr. Parker? His wife?

Sarah?

Had her first missive ever reached London?

She slid the message into a pouch hanging from her corset and took a moment to inspect her TTX weapon. Overreacting? No. Her training had taught her it was better to take precautions when one's nervous system sent out an alert, and from the way the hairs on the back of her neck quivered... The Parkers were an odd bunch, but Piyali could think of no obvious reason they would wish to interrupt her communications.

Hand loosely poised by her hip, she slid down the stairs. Only a few bleary-eyed regular drunks occupied a dark corner beside the peat fire on the hearth. Sarah leaned on the window sill, staring out at the street. Her parents were nowhere to be seen. Careful to move silently, Piyali ducked under the countertop and crept on her toes toward the Parkers' private quarters. If challenged, she would insist Mrs. Parker required medical evaluation.

For now, she listened at the door, to the cadence of what became increasingly hostile voices. Ever so carefully, she nudged the door ajar.

"What more do you want me to do?" Mrs. Parker grumbled. "I have it."

"What of the plant?" the innkeeper challenged.

Mrs. Parker huffed. "A cutting."

"Not good enough." Contempt laced his voice. "We need roots."

"They've killed every live sample we've sent," she snapped. "What good are roots? This time will be different. *We* take them the vine. *They* send a botanist to the rainforest to dig up an entire plant. We need to go. Now."

"No. Not with Sarah injured," he objected. "Besides, there might be further instructions."

There was a long silent pause in which Piyali imagined they glared daggers at each other.

"You want her cured," Mrs. Parker accused. "Yet you're quite happy to leave me to my fate. After all these years together, you'd sacrifice the queen to save the pawn?"

"I'm not the one who declined treatment."

"I overheard them. The ointment merely slows down the inevitable. Excision is the only cure. With that woman set upon recruiting help from London, we need to leave."

"Then shall I sharpen the knife?" Bitterness honed his words. "For amputation at your elbow is now your only opinion. The more natural joints you preserve, the better the prosthetic will function."

Mrs. Parker snarled back, her words too guttural and mangled for Piyali to understand. No, she realized, not distorted at all. The Parkers now argued in Russian.

Scrofula. They were both spies. Russian spies! Here. Living in the countryside of Wales—according to Sarah—for some years, establishing a cover, raising a daughter, biding their time. Realization dawned. If Mr. Black and Lister University wished to recruit Evan, so too would the Russians. Encouraging—*forcing*—Sarah to pursue him as a husband was a most excellent strategy.

Mrs. Parker must have been the one to break into Evan's home, leaving the greenhouse door ajar, rearranging shelf items. Sloppy of her. But what, exactly, had they taken? They'd had three long months since Evan returned from Brazil. The list could be quite long, even if they'd taken pains to steal only small samples of his specimens and tiny fractions of his supplies.

Piyali swallowed hard. They must know she was more than a physician. Why else steal her punch cards? This cast Mr. Black's silence in a different light. Had the tavern's rusty skeet pigeon ever taken flight?

Slowly, carefully, silently, she backed away. Evan's worst fears were about to become reality, but not at all via the channels he'd expected.

She needed to tell him. Now.

E van scraped his hand through his hair.

Over the past several hours, a gnawing sense of desperation had overtaken him. The latest development— free-swimming parasites infesting Seren's Well—had escalated the situation beyond anything he could hope to control. If he couldn't produce a solution, a cure, there would be no choice but to agree to summon Mr. Black and his agents, a most unwelcome conclusion to his struggles. While Lister University might be able to develop a cure, his secret would be in the hands of the British government.

He tried to imagine a positive outcome, but none of the scenarios his mind constructed ended well. Blue-skinned men—or women—with the ability to become invisible, an uncontrollable ability that was entirely subject to the whim of their emotional state. The government would ignore this unfortunate fact and try to mold such individuals into agents, to employ them for the greater good of the British Empire. But when inevitable madness resulted, what then? These agents would go rogue and disaster would result.

No. There was no alternative. A remedy had to be found.

"Copper," he announced to the empty room as a flash of insight struck.

Turning on his heel, he stared at the bottle of blue vitriol—copper sulfate to be exact. Though it was a substance often used to treat skin diseases, it hadn't proven equal to the task of eradicating the parasite. Neither had a *khu-neh-ari* preparation optimized for maximum naphthoquinone content.

However, analysis of the *khu-neh-ari* vine had also revealed the liana possessed an unusually high copper content. What would happen if he supplemented, rather than reduced the copper content of the new ointment?

Minutes later, an alcohol lamp burned at the base of a ring stand beneath a beaker containing the *khu-neh-ari* preparation, a yellowish, gel-like substance. Above the flask, a clamp held a glass volumetric burette filled with blue copper sulfate.

Evan stirred the ointment in the beaker with a glass rod until it melted. Then, slowly, he turned the burette's tap, allowing a drop of the blue liquid to fall into the yellow solution. Drip by drip, the *khu-neh-ari* absorbed the blue vitriol, gradually turning a reddish-brown as the mixture became more acidic.

Time to place his hypothesis to the test. After pipetting a measure of this new mixture into a Petri dish containing contaminated well water, there was nothing left to do but wait.

Staring at the hands of his pocket watch, he paced the flagstone floor—and lasted all of ten minutes. If this worked, if he could exterminate the parasites in the fairy well, then Mr. Black would not need to be summoned. That would win him additional time for further experimentation, time to determine a method by which to kill the creatures that crept beneath his skin.

But he was getting ahead of himself. First things first.

Recalling how Piyali had operated the aetheroscope, he prepared a slide and slid it into the aether chamber. A hiss. A process of focusing upon the specimen, gradually increasing the strength of the objective until the parasites came into focus.

For a moment, he forgot to breathe. Not a single one of the unicellular parasites moved, all floated motionless inside the small drop of fluid. A number of the wee creatures had lysed—burst—and fragments of their intracellular organelles were strewn about the field of vision.

Heart pounding, he leapt to his feet, knocking over the chair behind him in his haste to return to the solution-filled beaker. With a shaking hand, he lifted an eyedropper to extract a single drop of the anti-parasitic solution. He forced himself to take several long, steadying breaths—in and out—until his shimmering hand returned to a regrettable, yet familiar, blue.

He touched a drop of solution to the skin on the back of his hand and stared intently, praying, hardly daring to hope that it might penetrate the many layers of his skin to eradicate the creatures that burrowed within. Shock, then euphoria, rippled through him as a circle of blue color began to fade, slowly returning to a more normal, flesh-colored shade.

ANNE RENWICK

Whooping, he leapt to his feet, a wide grin stretching across his face as he strode across the room toward the door to snatch his coat from its hook. He needed to find Piyali, needed to pull her into his arms, spin her about and make plans for their future.

But before his hand could wrap about the handle, the door burst open and Piyali herself rushed into his cottage, wide-eyed and frantic. Her clothes were rumpled and several strands of hair had pulled free from her normally sleek braid. She slammed the wooden door behind her and fell backward against it, dragging in long, ragged breaths.

"What's wrong?" Worry shoved excitement to the floor.

"Spies," she panted, staggering forward. He caught her by the shoulders. "You've been living in a nest of them."

"Spies?" He lifted an eyebrow. "In Aberwyn, Wales?"

"The Parkers," she said.

As he listened to the rush of words that poured from her mouth, Evan began to pace. Her discovery reframed every interaction he'd had with them these last three months. As the proprietor of The White Hare, Mr. Parker had received and signed for every single item he'd shipped from Brazil during his expedition. Many of those crates had arrived before he himself even set foot on the dirigible that had carried him home to Britain. He'd not have noticed a few missing grams of dried Tawari tree bark or a few milliliters of Wasai extract.

And his plants... Once he'd begun to propagate them here, a missing seedling or two he would have overlooked as a failure to germinate or root in British soil.

Evan turned on his heel. An inventory of his stores, of his plants, might reveal discrepancies, but how could he—at this late date—hope to pinpoint exactly what was stolen? "Wait." His mind finally caught up with Piyali's words. "Did you say they pushed Sarah to seduce me?" Her constant flirtations, her wandering hands and the ever-present overflowing bosom accidentally brushing against him at any and every opportunity.

She nodded. "Though I don't think she knows her parents are Russian. I think she went along with the plan to wriggle out from under their thumb."

"Instead it would have tightened the noose about my neck." He strode to the tabletop, slapped a small square of paper upon it and lifted a fountain pen. "We need to send Mr. Black a message. Inform him of the spies and request backup. But whatever you do, don't mention the frog."

"What? We can't. Weren't you listening?" Her voice rose in volume.

"I'm sorry. Too much, too fast." His mouth fell open as she repeated herself. "Even if we trusted Mr. Parker to toss the clockwork contraption into the air, he has stolen all my pre-punched direction cards."

He looked pointedly at the pistol strapped to her hip. "Then we handle this ourselves."

"I suppose I could shoot them both, then bind them hand and foot," Piyali grumbled. "Heave them both in your crank wagon and haul them to Cardiff. From there I could contact headquarters, send them a cryptogram over the wire."

He snorted. "Dr. Piyali Mukherji, bounty hunter."

"Oh?" Her eyebrows rose. "You don't think I could?"

"I don't doubt it for a minute. I'll help. But first we ought to cure this infection."

"Evan," she said, shoving a few loose strands of hair behind her ears. "We're out of time. If they escape your village and turn this over to their handlers—"

"Let me rephrase," he interrupted. "While you slept the afternoon away, I found the cure." He no longer felt as if a spotted jaguar hunted him in the night. Once again the future held promise of happiness.

"A cure!" She rushed to the table, but its surface was clear. "What is it? What worked?"

"Copper," he answered, pointing to the aetheroscope upon his desk. "Take a look." As she bent over to peer into the aetheroscope, he explained. "You were right to suggest chemicals. Blue vitriol added to a *khu-neh-ari* preparation optimized for maximum naphthoquinone content. Neither works alone, but together, the copper multiplies the effect of the ointment."

She straightened. A wide smile lit up her face, her eyes. "This means we can treat the fairy well."

"Not quite." He waved a hand at his shelves. "I've not a fully-stocked pharmacy here," he reminded her. "Just a small bottle of copper sulfate. We'll need to make more."

"Simple enough. A couple copper farthings, some sulfuric acid, hydrogen peroxide, a little electricity courtesy of a strong battery..."

"Exactly. For now, the resulting preparation is rather watery, more of a tonic than an ointment, but there's more." He lifted the eyedropper. "Watch."

Holding out his hand, blue but for one small spot, he touched another drop of the solution to the skin on the back of his hand. Piyali stared intently, her eyes widening as a second circle of blue color began to fade, slowly returning to a more normal, flesh-colored shade.

"A biopsy," she demanded, breathless. "We need unambiguous confirmation. Have you performed one?"

"Not yet." He handed her a scalpel.

Piyali took a deep, calming breath, performed the procedure and inserted the slide into the aetheroscope. A moment later she pressed a hand to her heart and looked up at him with tears in her eyes. "Cured," she announced, then flung her arms about his neck, hugging him tight.

His—their—entire future, saved.

He wrapped his arms about her waist, ignoring the various attachments of her stiff leather corset that jutted into his skin. "With the entire fairy well infested, we'll need more of it than I have on hand in this bottle, but I've copper and acid and the *khu-neh-ari* liana grows quickly... with a touch of effort, we should be able to generate enough for our needs without traveling to Cardiff." He slid his hands lower, spreading his fingers wide over the curve of her backside. Her soft breasts pressing against his chest made it impossible to concentrate. "Perhaps, before we set to work, we could celebrate."

CHAPTER TEN

"Oh, is there something in particular you'd like to do?" Piyali kissed the rough edge of his jaw in encouragement. Now was not the time to speak of their future, but instead to celebrate that they once again had one, one that they would share together. Applying her fingers to the buttons of his shirt, she spread the coarse linen wide and hummed in appreciation as she ran her palms over the strong muscles and crisp hairs that lay beneath.

"As if you need to ask." He unfasted the metal buckles of her corset and stripped away the leather barrier that encircled her waist. Sliding his hands beneath the hem of her *choli*, he skimmed his palms over her rib cage before pulling the garment down her arms and dropping it to the floor. "I've not been able to stop thinking about you, about us."

She stood still as he caught a loose strand of her hair between his fingertips and drew its silky length forward across her shoulder. The backs of his fingers caressed the curve of her breast and her nipple tightened under his appreciative gaze. Then something in his eyes shifted. "I should have written sooner. The time we've lost..."

Brushing the pad of her thumb across his lips, she said, "I should have sent another skeet pigeon. And another. Until an entire flock pecked at your windows and compelled a reply. Forgive me?"

"Always."

Catching his lips with hers, she poured every ounce of her love into her kiss. Barriers crumbled between them, but Piyali refused to allow the tears that pricked at her eyes to ruin the pure joy of this moment. She held still as he pushed her away, tugging the string free from the end of her braid. He ran his fingers through her hair until it fell in loose waves, covering her shoulders and cascading down her back.

Only then did she step forward to peel back the collar of his shirt and press her lips to the soft skin of his neck where his pulse throbbed and tendrils of blue skin glimmered. "I've a request," she said, her voice once again light and teasing.

"Anything." His hands encircled her waist, urging her closer until the hard column of his shaft pressed against her stomach.

"A final request of sorts."

Worried eyes lifted to hers. "Final?"

"A final... performance for your hand." Her face burned at the erotic image that rose to mind. "I want to see it—or not—as it moves over my skin." Watching and not seeing, as if surrendering to a sensual dream.

His answering laugh was a low rumble. "Look down, then. Watch."

She lowered her gaze as his work-roughened left hand—in all its iridescent beauty—slid upward over her ribs to lift the weight of her breast in his palm. Something scraped the tip of her nipple—his fingernail—but she saw almost nothing. Everything was pure sensation. The roll of her flesh between his invisible thumb and forefinger. A delicious pinch sending a jolt of heat through her core.

"Evan!" she cried out as heat flooded her center, and her hips bucked against his. Then his mouth descended upon her other breast, sucking its tip deep into wet heat. "More," she demanded.

His hands left her breasts and cupped her buttocks. In one smooth motion, Evan lifted her into the air and strode across the room. Her backside landed upon the scarred, wooden table. He yanked the slippers from her feet and dragged off her skirt. "Not once did I ever imagine you spread like a feast upon my table." His eyes glinted darkly as they raked down her body. "But now that you're there..." He spread her knees apart, a glint of mischief in his eyes. "Don't forget to watch."

An unseen hand swept across her thigh, his finger slipping along her wetness, gently circling her nub. "Aether," she whispered, falling back onto her hands and arching her back when he plunged an invisible finger inside. In. Then out. And in. Her eyes fluttered shut.

"You're forgetting to look," he said, dark laughter in his voice. She forced her eyes open. The pressure inside her increased—a second finger joining the first—and then the base of his hand pressed hard against her mound.

Her hips bucked. *Enough.* Clawing at his waistband, she unfastened his trousers and shoved them down over his hips. "I want you inside me."

"So soon?" he asked. "I thought—"

"Now." Encircling his thick, hard length with her fingers, she drew forth a groan.

The pressure from his fingers slid away. A moment passed as he dug into his pocket, then a paper wrapper tore, and he covered himself. Rough hands dragged her hips to the edge of the wooden table. She lowered herself backward onto her elbows and wrapped her legs around his bare backside, urging him closer.

The head of his cock notched against her center. He gripped her hips and took her with one powerful thrust of his hips. *Yes. That.* That was the pressure she craved. Filled, stretched. Claimed by the man she loved.

"God, you're perfect." He retreated, then surged forward again. Over and over.

It wasn't enough. She wanted him closer. Needed him. She caught the free edges of his shirt and dragged him down on top of her. The crisp hairs of his chest rasped against her nipples, sending a tremor across her skin. The table beneath her grated against the floorboards, shifting with each passionate thrust, a potent expression of desire.

"Yes, Evan," she cried. "Don't stop." She lifted her knees higher, tipping her pelvis and twining her legs about his thighs to pull him deeper.

He grasped her hips, increasing the angle of his thrusts to rub harder against her center. His hot mouth fell against her neck, a gentle bite that left her mewling.

"Piyali," he rasped. "Come for me."

Her nails dug into his backside as a desperate tension built inside her and at last burst free. "Evan!" She cried out as tremors rolled over her, muscles clenching around increasingly frenzied thrusts. With a yell, he stiffened, driving himself into her one last time.

Sense returned slowly. Slowly, lazily, she opened her eyes and smiled. "How many feet did we travel?"

Laughing, he stabbed his fingers into her hair and gave her a long kiss before straightening. "Three?" Lifting her into his arms, he carried her upstairs to his bed, laying her upon its soft surface. "Tables might have their points, but beds…" He climbed in beside her, and she draped an arm across his chest, resting her head on his shoulder. His fingers trailed through her hair and she let her mind drift away as he murmured into her hair. "Once we eradicate this parasite, the Queen's agents never need know about any of this."

On the edge of sleep, his words shattered her euphoria. "What?" She bolted upright, clutching the sheet to her chest. "You still think there's no need to inform Mr. Black?"

"Exactly that," Evan replied.

"It's too late to hide what happened. Besides, he has ways of making people talk. When I bring them in, the Parkers will tell him everything. As will Tegan and her family. I'd look like a fool." Her career would never recover. How could he ask this of her? She climbed from the bed, wrapping the sheet about her. "Impossible."

"Why?" he countered, missing her warmth, even though the blaze of her narrow-eyed stare threatened to incinerate him. "Without the parasite, there's no risk of further infection. Once we treat the pool..." He trailed off, knowing they were at an impasse.

"Not so. Even after it's treated, the contaminated well water will need to be monitored on a regular basis to be certain the parasite does not take on a cyst form. Some unicellular organisms can survive months in cold water in such a state. To do that, my laboratory will need to know what to look for and how to identify the particular organism involved. I've no choice. Mr. Black must be informed."

She was right. Even if she agreed to hide the events of the past few days, Mr. Black would learn of them during an interrogation of the Parkers. He asked her to jeopardize both her career as a Queen's agent and the laboratory she'd been granted at Lister University. Not something he had the right to do.

"No." Piyali sliced a hand through the air. "I'll have no part in concealing this." She shot down the stairs.

The sheet from his bed made a soft *swoosh* as its loose end trailed downward. He yanked on a pair of trousers, grabbed a clean shirt and followed. "If we can wipe it out entirely, it won't fall into the wrong hands," he entreated.

Already she was half-dressed and pulling on her slippers. "Better to make a full report in the event that someone—hostile or friendly—encounters this infection again."

"Government has a way of abusing scientific advances," he countered, buttoning his shirt then reaching for his boots.

"True." She buckled her corset about her waist. "But who's to say the Russians haven't already been informed of this blue frog and the effects of its bite? Or whether or not they take the Parkers' reports seriously? Even if they don't have a sample yet, they're going to know where to send their people to look. Tracking your movements through Brazil can't possibly be that difficult. We take the frog into custody and record the cure. Better to be prepared, than to be caught unawares."

Evan pressed his lips together. They would never agree. Though he didn't relish the task, better for the blue frog to die, than to fall into the hands of Lister's research scientists. Not that that would stop herpetologists from hunting out more of its kind in Brazil. Perhaps he could simply soak the creature in the cure and deny this entire incident? He grabbed the flask of copper and *khu-neh-ari* extract. Pouring a generous amount into the palm of his hand, he began to rub the solution over his arm.

Piyali lifted an empty, lidded jar and strode into his greenhouse.

"Leave the creature here," he objected, following in her wake. "You can't possibly apprehend two Russian agents and keep the frog safe at the same time."

"If I leave it here, will you guarantee the frog won't disappear for good?" she asked, her expression growing suspicious.

Guilty intentions made him glance away. He'd make no such promises.

"I didn't think so." She bent before the terrarium squinting through the glass, searching for a hint of the frog. Unable to locate it, she heaved a sigh. "Can *you* see it?"

"Rather the point of being invisible, isn't it?" The greenhouse door was closed, secured with the 3XR CinchBolt. Still, he too stared through the glass. Not with the intent of handing it over but worried the frog had somehow escaped once again despite the heavy pharmacology textbook he'd placed on the terrarium's lid. He saw nothing blue. Nor was there a telltale pink and silver shimmer. Not even a frog-shaped blob reflecting the green of the terrarium's plant life. A cold tendril of fear wrapped around his spine.

"Stand back." If anyone was going to be bitten again, it was going to be him. Setting aside the textbook and shifting the lid, Evan reached inside. He felt nothing. When was the last time he thought to look for the frog? Yesterday. Before he plucked Sarah from Seren's Well. "What *exactly* did Mrs. Parker claim she'd taken?"

A faint knocking began at his cottage door, one that grew more frantic by the moment.

"A plant cutting. But she also said, 'I have it.' Do you think she meant the frog?" Piyali clamped a hand across her mouth, her eyes wide. "*That's* why she was unavailable last night to attend her daughter. If they've been watching you—us—then they know our every move. Mrs. Parker must have stolen the frog while we dealt with the aftermath of the fairy well altercation."

A trained agent would able to pick his lock. It was a probable scenario. His heart crashed into his ribs, then took off at a breakneck speed. "Yes." Sweat gathered at his temples. "I've no intention of handing over this frog to the Crown so they might seek out more of its kind. But I won't have the Russians run away with it either, and I'm ninety-nine percent certain it's not in this terrarium. They must have it already."

A face pressed up against the window of the greenhouse wall. Sarah. She slapped her palm repeatedly against the glass, shaking the metal frame. "Help!" she yelled. Tears streamed down her face. "You have to help me!"

Evan darted to the greenhouse door, unlocking and yanking it open. "What is it?"

Sarah fell into his arms, sobbing against his chest.

"Beginning to be a bit of a pattern, all these girls throwing themselves at you." Piyali's lips twisted as she reached out and pried Sarah free, steering her by the shoulders into the cottage. "Come sit. Mr. Tredegar has a new treatment to apply, a guaranteed cure. Your ankle will be fine." She pushed Sarah into a chair. "In the meantime, I have questions." She reached for Sarah's foot.

For months, the flirting had been relentless. Sarah and Tegan were too self-involved to realize his heart was sworn elsewhere. But Sarah wasn't one to cry crocodile tears. "It's not her ankle," he said with gut-twisting certainty.

"It's my mother," she keened, dragging in great gulps of air. "He killed her."

"Excuse me?" Piyali's hands froze on Sarah's stocking. "Explain."

"My father," Sarah cried, dashing away tears that would not stop falling. "They were fighting. It was awful. Worse than usual." Large glistening eyes blinked up at Piyali. Gasping for air, she struggled to control her breath enough to speak. "My mother was yelling about you being more than just a doctor. About how they were going to be locked away and tortured. She grabbed the teakettle from the kitchen range, shaking it at him and said something in a strange, foreign language. I've never seen my father look so angry. He raised his fist and struck her." A fresh deluge of tears poured down her cheeks. "Her head hit the corner of the table." A rattling gasp. "Blood. There was so much blood. And she didn't move. Father yelled at me to ready the steam cart, but I ran here instead."

"He needs to be stopped." Piyali's hand landed on her TTX pistol. She tugged it free, checking its readiness, before returning it to her holster.

"First we treat her ankle," Evan ordered as he lifted the bottle of copper and *khu-neh-ari* extract. The situation was escalating out of control. He wouldn't have this infection leaving his village. In any form. "It will only take a minute."

Piyali threw him a narrow-eyed glance, but yanked down Sarah's stocking and unwrapped the bandage about her ankle to reveal a glittering laceration. He soaked a cotton ball with the copper-liana tonic, then swabbed the liquid along the length of the suture. Corking the bottle, he shoved it into his pocket and yanked Sarah to her feet. "Grab the gauze," he ordered Piyali. "We'll bandage her later."

After running from the cottage to a nearby shed, Piyali jumped into the passenger's seat as he heaved Sarah into the bed of the wagon. Furiously, he cranked the vehicle to life.

"Hang on!" he yelled. Then, leaping into the driver's seat, he jerked the break free and rammed the driveshaft into full forward. The crank wagon took off like a shot, its wheels clattering over the many stones that studded the packed-earth lane that led down the hill and into the village.

CHAPTER ELEVEN

Her teeth nearly rattling out of their sockets, Piyali clutched the edge of her seat while Evan took the corner onto the main street on two wheels. There, in front of The White Hare stood a steam cart, puffing as it idled with Mr. Parker at its side. He took one look at their approaching vehicle and flung the valise he held into the cart before climbing behind the wheel.

"Father, no!" Sarah screamed.

Mr. Parker didn't so much as glance over his shoulder. The cart sprung to life, tearing down the muddy, rutted road. Villagers scattered, shaking their fists and cursing.

Evan followed.

Mr. Parker's loaded steam cart rattled and clanged as he fled, its loose contents bouncing above the rim, tossing the occasional paper-wrapped parcel onto the grassy verge of the road. One item jolted loose, but didn't fall free: Mrs. Parker's heavily bandaged arm. It hung limp, swaying and jerking with the motion of the vehicle, a grim reminder that Piyali was in pursuit of a man not deterred by death. Did he seek to hide his crime? Or was the corpse of his wife no more than a sample of an infectious disease to be delivered to his superiors, a gruesome commitment to his orders?

Sarah cried out in distress.

Piyali drew her weapon, but they were too far away. "Closer!" she yelled.

"This wagon doesn't go any faster," Evan yelled back. "But he'll have to slow down to take an upcoming turn. If I leave us at full speed, we can overtake him just before we run off the road. If we pursue him, we'll likely lose the race."

In short, the wagon's fully loaded steam hopper would allow it to outrun a crank cart. She couldn't take the chance. "Don't slow down," she yelled back.

"Get ready!" He gripped the driveshaft with white knuckles.

Ahead the road reversed course in a tight hairpin turn, a turn necessary to descend the steep hillside. The steamstage had slowed considerably with its approach to Aberwyn; Mr. Parker barely engaged the brakes.

Bouncing down the rough road on iron-rimmed wheels, Piyali raised her arm, sighting along the length of her TTX pistol. Three darts were loaded. One to stun. Two to render a man unconscious. A third would kill.

Mr. Parker was a large man, and she prayed only a single dart would be required.

"Now!" Evan yelled.

Time seemed to slow as they shot past the steam cart. Careening about the tight turn, Piyali squeezed the trigger. With a whoosh of compressed air, the dart shot forth, striking Mr. Parker directly between the shoulder blades. He howled in anger.

The front wheels of Evan's wagon ran off the road, jolting time back to its proper speed. The vehicle bucked, tossing Piyali free. Hours of training had her tucking into a roll. She hit the ground hard, and her body exploded into pain. Despite the screaming protest of every joint, she forced herself onto her feet and began to run across the muddy grass, back onto the road, pistol firmly in hand.

Mr. Parker's shoulders sagged forward, his hands sliding down the driving wheel as the cart careened down the hillside. Lungs heaving, heart pounding, she chased after him, grateful for her raised hemline. Though the sharp edges of gravel stabbed into the soles of the soft slippers she wore, she could not stop now.

She slid to a halt and gasped for air, trying to steady her arm as she took aim. She fired. The second dart grazed his neck. *Schistosomiasis!* If any of the neurotoxin had entered his system, a third would kill him. Still, better to chance it. To let him escape was unthinkable.

Planting her feet firmly upon the ground, she fired a third and final dart into his arm. Mr. Parker slumped sideways on his seat, then fell, disappearing from view. *Excellent.* Evan ran past her, hauling himself into the cart and yanking on the breaking mechanism. By the time she arrived, he had already dragged Mr. Parker— still breathing—from the cart.

Sarah collapsed at her father's side in a heap. "Will he live?" she asked as Piyali unhooked a pair of manacles from her corset and shackled his wrists.

"Yes." For now. Once Mr. Black took him into custody, she could make no promises.

Face contorted in a mixture of anger and concern, Sarah lifted a shaking hand then laid it upon her father's chest. "And my mother?"

"Dead," Evan answered her simply.

Leaving Sarah to struggle with her grief, Piyali took a deep steadying breath. There was no avoiding it. Mrs. Parker must be examined, the contents of the wagon bed searched. She pulled herself onto the running board. It was impossible to pry her eyes from Mrs. Parker's ghastly remains. The back of her head was caved in, clots of blood matted her hair. Her arm was wrapped in yards of dingy gauze that took Piyali several long minutes to unwind. Exposed to the light of day, Mrs. Parker's arm was not only a scintillating blue, but her hand had swollen to twice its normal size. Untreated, blood poisoning—septicemia—had also taken hold.

Beside her, Evan let out a low whistle. "Murdered, yes, but even so, there's little chance she would have reached Russia alive."

"The frog," she said. They needed to secure the creature.

Evan pried the lid off one of the many crates. Inside, padded with straw, lay several glass jars labeled with his own handwriting. A second crate held dried plant cuttings carefully pressed and wrapped in paper. He dug through a third, then a fourth. All filled with a variety of materials stolen from his greenhouse and laboratory. "Quite the collection they made this past year. To think that I never suspected a thing until the blue frog escaped."

Frantic, Piyali dug through the remaining crates. "It has to be here..." A soft, plopping sound came from a copper teakettle tucked into the straw. Why would anyone pack a teakettle whilst fleeing for Russia? Frowning, she plucked it free. The teakettle was heavier than it ought to be, far heavier than could be accounted for by the addition of a small frog. As she shifted the kettle and reached for its lid, something inside scraped noisily across its base.

"Wait!" Even cried. He dug into the straw and then emptied a glass jar of its contents. "Slowly and carefully." He held the jar close as Piyali pried free the kettle's lid and peered inside.

At first glance all she saw was a thin film of water and shards of the white ceramic pot she'd handed to Sarah, the container of *khu-neh-ari* ointment. But then the light glinted off two small, beady eyes. A dazed and confused frog. She tipped it gently into the glass jar. It looked exactly like the one they had trapped at Seren's Well.

Except it wasn't blue.

"It's green," Evan said, eyebrows knitting in confusion.

"Cured?" And then all the tension melted away as she began to laugh. Gallows humor, perhaps, but the two Russian spies had managed to steal so much, yet botched it in the end. "So close to success, but..." She examined the kettle, then held it up. "A copper teakettle to provide a damp habitat for the frog—not the worst plan. But add in a jar of your ointment and a rough wagon ride through the Welsh countryside..."

"And the frog itself is cured," Evan finished.

Had the Parker's plans not been disrupted—with more time to pack and pad the stolen goods—they might have reached the port of Cardiff with intact specimens. With a ship ready and waiting, there was a small chance the spies and a blue frog would have reached Russia. And then...

No. It didn't bear thinking about.

Evan braced as Piyali straightened and dragged in a deep breath. "The Parker family must be delivered into Mr. Black's custody along with any documents found in their private apartments." Her voice held an edge that informed him she would tolerate no further objections.

"Agreed."

Surprise lifted her eyebrows. "But concerning the blue frog and my report..." She set down the teakettle and brushed a piece of straw from her tunic. "I propose a compromise."

"Go on," he prompted. He wanted to reach out and gather her into his arms, but knew he could not. Terms were being set. There was no avoiding Mr. Black or his men now. A lump of coal burned in his stomach. What kind of future could they have together if they could not find common ground?

"Before the Queen's agents arrive, I propose we soak Mrs. Parker's arm in the copper-liana solution. We treat both Tegan and the water in Seren's Well. If this works, if we can eliminate all traces of the parasite, I will petition Mr. Black to allow me to personally monitor the pool for the next several years. Mr. Black and the Queen's agents would receive nothing more than a report about the parasite itself, excluding its origin. I won't include a single reference to the frog." She cleared her throat. "It will, of course, mean convincing everyone that Tegan fabricated the story concerning a certain blue amphibian."

Dark eyes met his. Was Piyali holding her breath as she waited for his response? Did she envision a future which included him? What an amazing woman, one who could be his if he too made this small concession. The infectious parasite would not be preserved, living or dead, but it would be carefully documented along with its cure, a cure he would quietly share with the shaman of the village that had hosted him in Brazil. The Crown would *not* be provided with the means to create semi-invisible men, but neither would Lister biologists be left with no identification or treatment particulars should the intracellular parasite ever resurface.

"Tegan will never speak to me again, but I'll manage." With a light heart, he caught her shaking hand, pressing it between his palms. "If I augment that report with a living specimen of the *khu-neh-ari* liana, will you personally recommend me for the position of Director of Tropical Plants in the Lister Botanical Gardens and Greenhouse? I've a sudden desire to relocate to London."

A wide smile brightened Piyali's face. Her eyes sparkled as she answered, "Absolutely."

"Curing unknown tropical diseases, uncovering entrenched Russian spies, firing poisonous darts with deadly precision." He drew her close. "What other mad skills have you acquired these past years?"

Her smile turned coy as her arms slid around his waist. "I'm afraid you'll need government clearance to find out. Have you ever considered working for the Queen?"

"I believe I could be persuaded," he said, then lowered his lips to hers.

The rest of the evening passed in a blur. Sarah, alternately weeping over the death of her mother and railing at her father, was returned to her room at The White Hare. Although they took the precaution of locking her door, neither he nor Piyali considered her a flight risk. Mr. Parker, however, was kept securely restrained and administered regular doses of laudanum to ensure he remained subdued.

Tegan was promptly treated. Clutching his hand and pressing it to her heart, she swore her undying love and loyalty. Until he mentioned that he expected to join Dr. Mukherji soon in London and wished her—and her parents—all the best here in Wales. At that unwelcome and unexpected news, her face soured, and she threw his hand back at him with a frustrated howl.

Together, he and Piyali searched the Parkers' living quarters, finding both her original message—still sealed in its tin cylinder—as well as the punch cards stolen from her trunk. Lips pursed in annoyance, Piyali dashed off a brief message informing Mr. Black that she had apprehended a Russian spy and required backup.

The White Hare's skeet pigeon, though rusty, had taken to the sky easily enough, winging its way to London. A strong response arrived the next day in the form of a silver-ballooned dirigible. The entire village turned out in the rain—jaws hanging open—to watch the unprecedented arrival of a hawk-class vessel descend from the sky and settle in the mud before the tavern.

Two men leapt from its compartment; neither were Mr. Black. With a glance of apology, Piyali left Evan's side, secreting herself behind closed doors to present her report. Disappointment tightened his chest, but he was not an agent. For the moment, he was nothing to the Crown but an importer of a biological hazard. Step one toward their future involved Piyali arguing on his behalf.

Several hours later, they emerged. Precious few words were exchanged as they began the process of loading evidence—including a potted sample of his liana—into a secure storage compartment of the airship's gondola. A few minutes before their scheduled departure, one of the men led Mr. Parker and Sarah in shackles from the tavern to securely bolt them into their seats.

Mr. Parker's lips pressed into a thin line. He stared stoically into the distance, refusing to acknowledge anyone or anything.

"How is it possible?" Sarah asked, her eyes red and swollen. Gone was her usual ebullience, squashed beneath the truth of her parents' lives. "Russian spies!"

"It's a lot to take in." Piyali placed a hand on her arm. "Cooperate. Answer all their questions truthfully and, if—when—you're cleared of all wrongdoing, I shall do my best to help you start a new life in London. I'll see your textbooks delivered to your cell. Focus on your studies to pass the time and improve your future prospects. When this is over, I'll do what I can to arrange for you to take the entrance exams for Girton's College."

As the airship departed, as all faces turned upward to watch its departure, Evan asked, "Is all well?"

"Mr. Black agreed to my proposal," she answered, tugging him by the hand down the main road and away from the crowd. "The pool is now your—our—responsibility."

Together, they slipped away into the woods. Piyali folded her arm through his as they came to a stop before Seren's Well. Its waters glistened a turquoise blue from all the copper sulfate they had poured into the pool, and branches from the *khu-neh-ari* liana floated on its surface.

Traditions transformed and evolved with time, and another step forward needed to begin today. While Piyali spoke with fellow Queen's agents, he'd spoken with Mr. Price, impressing upon him the need to return his supply of steel pins to the manufacturer, to request that only copper pins be sold in the village store. Even better if Evan could convince the villagers that the *gwragedd annwn* desired payment, not bent pins, in the form of copper farthings. The more copper introduced to the pool, the better.

"I've been granted three days leave," Piyali said, breaking the silence. "Three days to convince you that both you and your plants belong in the Botanical Garden of Lister University."

"Done," he said and reached into his coat pocket. Heart pounding, he lowered himself onto one knee and held up his grandmother's opal and diamond ring, a ring that had burned against his chest all day. "That leaves me three days to convince you to say yes. Dr. Piyali Mukherji, I cannot envision my future without you in it. These years without you nearly killed me. Will you do me the great honor of becoming my wife?"

A tear slid down her cheek as she slipped the ring on her finger. "Yes."

Her answer dispelled the gloom that had descended upon his life some three months past. Intensity of color rushed back into his life, leaving him breathless. Evan leapt to his feet and scooped her into his arms, turning toward his cottage. "How shall we spend the next three days? Planning a wedding? Packing the laboratory and the contents of my greenhouse..."

She tugged on his arm. "Anticipating wedding vows."

Keep reading for an excerpt of

THE GOLDEN SPIDER

The Elemental Web Chronicles — Book One

A stolen clockwork spider. A forbidden romance.
A murderous spy on the streets of London who
must be stopped before it's too late.

CHAPTER ONE

London, Fall 1884

The honor of working for the Queen as a spy was overrated.

Crouched behind a burned-out steam carriage, Sebastian Talbot, the 5th Earl of Thornton, tapped on the acousticocept wrapped about his ear. The device should have worked up to a half-mile distance. He squinted through the gloom of the riverside fog. Hell, he could still see their agent. He just couldn't hear him.

"No signal," he hissed to the man beside him. Would they ever manage to make this damn device work in the field?

His partner, Mr. Black, frowned. "Same."

"Repairs." Thornton pointed across the field of rusting scrap metal before them to a derelict water boiler just large enough to conceal both men in the dark of night. "There." After years of working side by side, the two men could almost read each other's minds.

Black nodded and they ran forward, tracing a winding path through piles of discarded machinery in an attempt to melt into the odd shadows the metal cast. Their agent was no more than fifty feet away, but Thornton still couldn't hear the conversation between Agent Smith and his informant. He threw Black a questioning look, but the man shook his head. Nothing.

Thornton bit back a curse. They couldn't approach Smith without blowing his cover.

Black ripped the acousticocept from his ear and twisted its dials in vain trying to increase reception. The light continued to blink red. Either the agent's artificial ear had failed or there was some fresh blunder with the receiver.

Thornton ran through the schematics in his mind. The aether chamber inside the agent's ear was sealed. Tests had proven that in the laboratory this afternoon. The next logical weak point was the needles contacting the counter rotating disks in the acousticocepts. They had a tendency to dislodge.

He wanted to growl in frustration. Henri should have fixed that problem by now. The device should be beyond field trials. They should have been sitting in a steam coach listening to the informant's tale in complete warmth and comfort, not running about a scrap yard straight from a debriefing at the opera and risking discovery in blindingly white shirts, snowy cravats, and well-tailored coats. Thornton kept a hand tightly wrapped over his silver-capped cane lest it reflect some stray ray of light and draw attention like a bioluminescent beacon.

And his leg was sending out pangs of warning. Damn sky pirate and his cutlass.

Thornton ignored the radiating pain. He pulled a cigarette case from his coat pocket as he stepped behind the metal tank. He raised his eyebrows at Black. Smith believed his informant finally had a solid lead. If Thornton didn't attempt field repairs, he and Black would be reduced to simple observation. Too many carefully woven plans had unraveled of late, and he did not relish the thought of delivering yet another report of failure to his superior.

Black nodded and angled his torso to further block any view of Thornton's activities. Flipping it open, he activated the small decilamp—its light a necessary risk— and selected micro-tweezers from among the various tools within. There was a chance he could reset the needles of the acousticocept before the agent moved to follow the informant's lead.

His cold fingers fumbled. Gloves. He'd been about to return for them when he'd spotted a determined mother steering her debutant daughter into his opera box. Discomfort, no matter how biting, was preferable to becoming trapped in such a snare. Warmth had been abandoned in favor of freedom.

Black shifted closer as Thornton pulled his acousticocept free and placed it on a steam gauge protruding from the boiler. Thornton flipped a monocle over his eye and, with only the faint blue-green light to illuminate the needles, set to work.

As always, the world about him faded as he untangled an experimental conundrum.

Moments later, the light glowed a steady green. Success, but no satisfaction. He'd uncovered yet another internal defect. Tomorrow, he would sketch out modifications to solve this issue once and for all. He handed the device to Black and set about fixing the second one. Hooking the working acousticocept once again about his ear, Thornton was drawn into the distant exchange.

"...how is the eye doctor making contact with the gypsies?" Smith asked.

The ragged informant shrugged. "I want nuthin' more to do with this so-called doctor. Got me two young'uns, I do. Can't be found floating down the Thames." He turned away.

"Wait..."

But the informant had already disappeared into the night.

There was a crunch of shoes on gravel. A soft splash followed. Then Smith spoke as if to himself, though the information was directed to them. "I'm going to investigate."

Thornton glanced at Black in question. The man shook his head. Because of the malfunctioning device, they'd missed a crucial piece of information.

Rising from behind the boiler, he caught sight of their agent—but not his informant. Smith had climbed into a boat and was rowing down the Thames. Risky, with the Thames' kraken population on the rise. But as long as Smith hugged the shoreline and avoided storm pipes, he might reach his destination—whatever that was—before the smaller kraken swarmed and sank the boat.

But where did that leave them? There was no way to flag down Smith without compromising him. He sagged against the boiler in frustration. At this dark and foggy hour the usual clamor of steam engines, sailors' calls and horns was muted, and through the acousticocept, he could hear the sound of waves lapping at a boat's hull.

So much for simple surveillance.

"There's a dock not far." Black glanced at Thornton's leg. "Can you make it?"

He narrowed his eyes. Such concern was unnecessary. For now. "I can make it."

"Or go down trying," Black retorted.

Before Thornton could snarl an appropriate response, Black was off and running. Using his cane to counterbalance his awkward gait, he followed across the mud and rock of the riverbank, cursing as he stepped on a decaying kraken carcass and nearly lost his footing. The beasts were everywhere, the stench from their decaying bodies rising to fill his nostrils.

By the time he reached said dock, Black was already casting away the ropes. "Hurry up, old man."

Thornton leapt into the boat, and a lightning bolt of pain shot through his leg.

As Black rowed in pursuit and shook free the occasional tentacle that hooked an oar, Thornton unscrewed the silver head of his cane and pulled a glass vial as well as a needle from within. With practiced movements, he fitted the vial with a small needle. Yanking a pant leg above his knee, he injected the contents.

Instant relief. He dragged in a deep breath and shoved the empty vial into his coat pocket.

"Better?" Black asked.

Thornton reassembled his cane and gave a terse nod. As the tension melted from his muscles, he scanned the water for their man. "There, by the warehouse."

Black adjusted course.

The drug's effectiveness wouldn't last. Once, a single dose had dulled the pain for an entire month. Now he needed to administer the drug daily. It was time to curtail his field duties further. Perhaps eliminate them altogether. Before an agent fell victim to his injury.

A bitter pill to swallow for a man in his early thirties.

In the distance, Smith effortlessly dragged the boat ashore and ducked inside the brick building. His footsteps echoed in Thornton's ear.

"There's a light," the agent whispered. "A faint tapping."

There was a rustle, the sound of a coat being pushed aside and the scrape of a weapon drawn. The agent screamed. An agonizing sound that had both Thornton and Black gripping their ears. An altogether too brief scream that ended with a gurgle. There was a loud crunch followed by telling static.

Though he and Black wore the acousticocept listening devices coiled about their ears, the transmitting device, the acousticotransmitter, had been implanted deep *inside* Smith's ear.

Pulling on the oars, Black beached the boat onto the muddy, trash-laden shore. They ran to the building. Not a single glimmer of light escaped its tall windows. Thornton yanked on the rusty door handle. "Locked."

"Stand back," Black ordered, then kicked the door open, entering with Thornton at his back. Both held their weapons at the ready.

Nothing but silence and their agent, sprawled on the ground—a faint trickle of blood oozing from his ear around a protruding stiletto blade—met their entry.

Thornton clenched his jaw and bent over. He avoided Smith's vacant eyes as he pressed fingers to the agent's throat in the unlikely event that he might find a faint pulse. Nothing. He looked upward, his gaze drawn to the other horror in the room.

Black had flicked on his bioluminescent torch. The cavernous riverside warehouse was filled with stacked wooden crates. In its center, over the delivery hatch in the dock that stretched out over the river, hung a block and tackle. Suspended from the iron hook by rope-bound hands was another man beyond rescue. Blood streaked down his face and neck, soaking the front of a saffron-colored shirt. Empty eye sockets stared down at them.

"Damn it," Black swore. "Not again."

CHAPTER TWO

The day began much like any other day.

Lady Amanda Ravensdale, daughter of the Duke of Avesbury, took a bite of buttered toast and a sip of cold tea before returning her attention to the femur resting before her on the polished mahogany dining table. A practical examination approached, and she had her heart set on achieving a perfect score. She scanned its surface, murmuring anatomical terms. Greater trochanter, medial epicondyle, linea aspera—

A grinding of gears and a gentle bump against her chair drew her attention. "Thank you, RT," she said to the steambot, lifting a china cup filled with fresh, hot tea. The roving table reversed course and whirred its way back toward the kitchens.

"Must you!" Olivia shrieked from behind her. "The horrors I endure each day as a member of this family. I will never forgive you for caving to such a base desire to mingle with the middle class in an anatomical theater. My sister in medical school. It's a social nightmare."

Amanda smirked at her sister's tantrum and twisted in her chair. "And I will never forgive you for the hours I've lost enduring soliloquy after soliloquy about the difficulties of obtaining an ice sculpture come June."

"I'll have you know planning a proper society wedding is quite an undertaking." Olivia pointed her nose in the air, and golden ringlets bounced about her face. "Carlton will one day be Viscount Bromwich."

"Children," Father warned from the end of the table. He lifted the morning paper higher. On the front page, headlines proclaimed the latest indignity: A German Imperial Fleet zeppelin had attacked what was, the British Navy insisted, a mere merchant's vessel.

"At least a wedding is a suitable pursuit for a lady," Olivia persisted as she stomped over to the buffet. "Carlton says women have no business pursuing a career."

Amanda rolled her eyes. She was thoroughly sick of hearing her future brother-in-law quoted, so she stuck in the proverbial scalpel and gave it a sharp twist. "Carlton simply wants nothing to distract you from your duty as brood mare."

Her sister's jaw unhinged, and she all but dropped her plate of dry toast on the table. "You are so crass.

It's to society's benefit that you've set course to become a dried up old maid."

"If that's what it takes to be permitted to use my talents." It wasn't that she opposed marriage. Or children. It was the limitations a husband imposed upon a married female member of the peerage. Not a single man had yet met her standards. "Though Mr. Sommersby shows promise," she added aloud. He was the only male classmate who didn't sneer at her presence in the lecture hall. Quite the opposite. Not that she had *feelings* for him, but she'd promised Father she would husband hunt.

"The second son of a baron. A mere commoner," Olivia sniffed, but when she turned toward Father, her expression grew concerned. "Speaking of marriage and rotten siblings, any news of Emily?"

Another manifestation of Olivia's obsession with marrying a title. Scandal might break at any moment. The *ton* believed Lady Emily visited relatives in Italy, but if society learned the truth—that their sister had run off with gypsies to study ancient herbal lore—well, Carlton wouldn't want anything to do with Olivia.

Worse, Emily had also married Luca, a gypsy she'd known since childhood—a fact she and Father had kept from the rest of the family. No need to send Mother and Olivia into a blind panic. Though Amanda herself was proud of her sister for taking her future into her own hands, Father's response was more tempered. He respected Emily's decision, but had three as-yet unwed children to manage and a wife who valued her social connections among the *ton* above all else. As such, all communication with her sister had been severed.

Father's narrowed eyes appeared over the top of the paper. "Not a word." He carefully folded the paper, placed it on the table and pointed to an article. "Though I worry for her every day."

Amanda leaned forward, reading over her sister's shoulder. There in all its gruesome detail buried at the bottom of page eight:

South London. Another gypsy slain, eyes torn from sockets. One must wonder to what he bore witness.

A small frisson of worry skittered down her spine. Luca's family often settled in South London during the coming winter months, and gypsies traveled in tightly knit family groups. She could only hope that this year his family had chosen another city.

Amanda stepped through the French windows of the library into the crisp, cool autumn air and strolled through the gardens toward the chicken coop. "A good morning to you, Penny," Amanda greeted a fat, white hen.

Penny clucked her usual cheerful response.

Eight years ago, the Town and City Food Act of 1876 had legislated that all homeowners, peers not excepted, contribute to the problem of city-wide food shortages. As duchess, Mother had decreed they would produce eggs rather than put her precious gardens to plow.

Amanda had appropriated the use of the coop's storage room as her laboratory and enlisted the orange-striped cat, Rufus, who now twined about her ankles, as her laboratory assistant. His duties included providing her with mice suffering from spinal injuries, patients obtained during their ill-fated night-time raids on the chicken feed. The cat followed as she moved to a door in the back wall where a lock was mounted. She dialed in a ten-digit security code. Tumblers fell into place and the door swung open.

Potentially useful items cluttered the room. Shelves of glassware, bottles and rubber tubing. Boxes of clockwork components. Stacks of papers and stubs of pencils.

Yet none of the contents mattered save one. On the wide workbench before her, a single cage rested. Inside, a tiny mouse tucked into cotton batting was curled on his side as if in deep sleep. For a brief moment, she held her breath and let herself hope. Perhaps that's all it was, sleep.

She crossed to the bench and bent to examine her patient, watching for the gentle rise and fall of the mouse's ribcage but saw no movement. Still, Amanda clung to hope. Perhaps he breathed shallowly due to the pain of the surgery. That she could ease.

Except there was a smear of blood on the cotton, a clear indication the surgery had failed. Again. Her heart sank.

Rufus leapt beside her and sniffed the mouse through the wire mesh of its cage, performing his own examination. He looked up at her with mournful golden eyes and let out a gut-wrenching yowl.

Dead.

Breakfast congealed into a hard lump in her stomach. She'd had such high expectations last night. Swallowing her disappointment and frustration, Amanda fell back on protocol. She opened the cage, scooping the small, cold mouse from his bedding and slid him into the aetheroscope's observation chamber to seal him from the outside atmosphere. She cranked the handle of the machine, sending concentrated aether though its pipes and valves while activating the vacuum chamber. The device, a birthday present from her brother Ned, replaced oxygen with aether, allowing her to resolve far smaller objects than her other microscope ever had, no matter its powerful objectives.

Perching on a stool, Amanda peered through the eyepiece and twisted the dials into focus. Rotating first one knob and then another, she brought the neuromuscular junction of the muscle into view and sighed. The connection had indeed failed.

Five years ago, after Ned's tragic accident stole the use of his legs, her life-long interest in medicine had found a clear focus. She'd concentrated her efforts on the neuromuscular system, conceptualizing and then building a neurachnid, a programmable, clockwork spider the size of a bronze halfpence, one that could spin a replacement for a damaged motor neuron following spinal injury.

It sat in a place of honor on a wooden shelf above her workbench. Eight long, hinged legs arched out from a finely mechanized clockwork thorax that controlled the weaving mechanism. Lodged in the abdomen were two other key features. A tiny slot for a miniature Babbage card to direct the neurachnid's activities and a small glass vial, a reservoir for a potent nerve agent administered as the spider worked. The patient's nerve fibers needed to be quieted, but not fully anesthetized, in order for the spider to trace the pathway of the damaged neuron and, using thin gold fibers, reconnect spinal cord to muscle and restore movement.

Last night, the neurachnid had successfully replaced a spinal motor neuron in this mouse. The patient had been able to extend his lower leg. He'd walked for an entire hour. She'd returned her patient to his cage, confident she would find him walking about the cage this morning.

He hadn't. It was still the same problem. The neuromuscular junction always failed to hold. And when a mouse discovered itself unable to walk, often it reacted by chewing at the fine gold wires, growing increasingly stressed until blood loss and panic simply overwhelmed the tiny creature.

Amanda sat back, punching a button to release the gasses. The microscope hissed and spat, echoing her frustration. She wanted to scream, to fling the spider against the wall and weep for all the hours lost in her futile efforts in this smelly, dim room barely worthy of the term laboratory. She took a deep breath and pushed away the urge.

If only she had a properly equipped laboratory and trained colleagues.

Instead, she picked up the small neurachnid from its shelf and racked her brain looking over the myriad gears and pins, clicks and rivets. If she only could deduce what the problem was, she could devise a solution. But it looked as it always had. She needed fresh eyes. She needed help, competent help that could provide a leap of insight.

She'd tried communicating by post, seeking help from notable neurophysiologists. Most ignored her missives outright, but the handful that responded suggested she abandon her project, citing its impossibility.

But it couldn't be impossible. And she wouldn't quit.

Ned *had* to walk again.

CHAPTER THREE

Thornton stood at the front of the lecture theater frowning as students filed into the room. The men jostled and shoved, laughing and joking as they crashed about, eventually managing to land in seats. He supposed he'd been much the same as them. Once.

Lister University School of Medicine, founded by the Queen as a co-educational institution to seek out the brightest young medical minds, had not yet managed to find an equal number of women who were capable of passing the rigorous academic exams required for admission. Only three women, all dressed in dark hues, filed into the back row of seats, perching there stiff and solemn, staring down at him intently, like a murder of crows. He distinctly recalled being told there were four women in this class. One of their number was missing.

What had the dean been thinking forcing him to take on this task? Thornton belonged in his laboratory, pressing the boundaries of neuroscience, consulting with the Queen's agents to stop a murderer who sought to turn Britain's own technology against them. Not stuffing anatomical facts into impenetrable brains.

Ordered by the Queen to the Orkney Islands to investigate a sudden spike in reported sightings of selkies off the coast, Corwin, professor of anatomy, had headed north late last night. The suspicion was that Iceland was dispatching altered Inuit for reasons yet to be determined. Thornton didn't envy the man the dark and cold October nights he would spend perched on the rocky coast. Nevertheless, it meant Professor Corwin required a replacement for the term, and Thornton's physical injuries were no longer considered sufficient excuse for him to avoid teaching obligations.

But lectures were just the start of it all. There would be students in his office asking all manner of questions. Most of them would be ridiculous. Both the questions and the students. So many of them couldn't think their way out of a paper bag. Even worse, there would be exams. Exams he would have to grade. Thornton sighed thinking of the sheer quantity of red ink he would require in the near future. Waste of his time, all of it.

He walked to the podium where the limelight lantern rested, glass projection slides of the human nervous system at the ready. He twisted the gas lines providing both oxygen and hydrogen into "on" positions, picked up the striker and lit the cylinder of quicklime.

There was a lull in the conversation. Thornton cleared his throat and looked up at his audience, expecting all eyes to have focused attentively upon him. Instead, he saw the backs of fifty odd heads and only one face.

A very beautiful face. One with deep pink lips, high cheekbones and a dainty nose between wide eyes that had just a hint of an exotic tilt. Smooth skin, all surrounded by elaborately coiffed hair the color of midnight. Unlike the crows in the back who rolled their eyes in disgust, this woman was garbed in the latest of fashions, a tightly corseted and bustled teal gown with a low cut neckline that had all the men leering.

All but him, of course.

Striking blue eyes met his gaze.

He lifted his eyebrows and drew out his pocket watch to consult the hour. It was five past. She was late.

Her lips curved upward at his obvious reprimand, but she made no effort to hasten her steps. A gentleman in the front row stood, gesturing to a vacant seat he clearly intended for her to occupy. She nodded in greeting, then with the twist of a knob at her waist to collapse her bustle, she removed her feathered hat and settled into the chair beside the smug-looking gentleman.

Instinct told Thornton she would be a problem. A woman with such obvious physical charms expected attention. Best to not provide it. He waved his hand at his assistant and the room plunged into darkness. Sliding home the first glass plate, an illuminated image appeared on the large screen hanging at the front of the hall.

Tomorrow, he would not wait. If she could not manage to arrive promptly, she could damn well stumble her way down the stairs or sit in the back.

"Neurons and glial cells," he intoned. "Later in the laboratory you will closely study the features of both."

A manda leaned forward in her chair, entranced by the deep, booming voice of this new professor. The light cast by the limelight lantern threw his angular face into sharp relief. What captivating facial bone structure. Prominent zygomatic arches and a long square jaw made the planes of his face appear wide and harsh. Between his dark eyebrows, nasal bones stretched into a long, straight and distinctive nose. Damp hair severely slicked back from his forehead betrayed the man by daring to curl at its tips. Full lips formed words in a tone that made the features of a neuron sound utterly entrancing.

She rather thought she could be content to spend the entire morning listening to him read the index of her anatomy text. Clearly brilliant, he was also the best physical specimen she'd laid eyes on in a long time. Too bad about that clause in the school's charter forbidding professors from entering into relationships with their students.

A flush rose upward across her face. Such thoughts. She forced her gaze to the projection on the screen. *Focus, Amanda.*

He was proceeding at such a rapid clip that she would soon be left behind if she could not pull her head out of the aether.

Though she put pen to paper, she could not stop herself from asking. "What happened to Professor Corwin?" she whispered to Simon, or Mr. Sommersby as she addressed him in public.

Simon shifted to lean his shoulder lightly against her own. Male instinct, she supposed, to mark her as his own. Behavior she'd encouraged. "No idea. But it seems Lord Thornton is to finish the lecture series."

Her indrawn breath was audible.

Lord Sebastian Talbot, Earl of Thornton and renowned neurophysiologist teaching a course! She'd known he was on staff, but it was rumored that he never lectured. Whatever forced him to the podium, she did not care. Fortune had finally smiled upon her. He might have ignored her attempts to open a scientific correspondence about the possibility of using gold filaments to conduct neurological impulses, but he could not ignore her physical presence in his office as his student.

Excitement must have shown in her face as she contemplated this unexpected windfall, for Lord Thornton's eyes flickered toward her. Did she detect surprise in the slight drawing together of his eyebrows? Hard to be certain, for his words never slowed. She had to convince him of the merit of her work. Convince him to allow her to demonstrate the function of her neurachnid, for his insight would be profound.

He'd already taken notice of her. Twice.

She winced. Not the best first impression. She had been late, and he'd sent quite the scowl in her direction.

If not for the overturned horse cart in the street—horses and steam coaches did not mix well—she would have been punctual. Amanda hated arriving late, enduring the disapproving stares of the other women, the speculative leers of the men. She'd fully intended to politely perch in the back. But when this new professor had met her gaze, seeming to challenge her right to enter, neither fire nor brimstone would have kept her from her usual center seat in the front row.

It was a matter of principle. She'd set a precedent she intended to uphold. Amanda was polite and collegial, stubbornly refusing to be relegated to the dark edges and corners of the room where most male classmates seemed to think she and the other three women belonged.

If only they'd join her.

Betsy, Joan and Sarah clung desperately to the notion that the best manner in which to succeed in medicine as a woman was to efface their sex with severely tailored dresses. Dark colors, long sleeves and high necklines revealing only the oval of their faces. They worked diligently at making themselves unpleasant and uncomfortable. Amanda saw no need to dress the dowd.

She took pride in her appearance, and if her ladylike and professional behavior set her apart from others, so be it.

Lord Thornton paced back and forth across the dim lecture hall, a slight hitch to his step, while expounding upon the wonders of the neurological system, changing glass slides with astonishing speed.

Like her classmates, Amanda wrote furiously, her hand cramping. But instead of directing her eyes to the projected images, she stole glances at the man.

With an emphatic wave of his arm, a lock of his hair began to free itself. Another followed. Curls began to assert themselves, twisting tighter and sending waves along each strand. Lord Thornton's hair took on a life of its own, falling across his brow in playful waves.

Though they'd never met, he was *ton* and rumors reached her ears at the various society events she'd been forced to attend. He'd been involved in a terrible dirigible accident, no doubt responsible for the slight limp she detected, but most of the gossip had centered upon his new-found eligibility. For unknown reasons, his long-time fiancée had jilted him mere months before their wedding. Not that any hopeful brides cared why. He was titled and therefore a matrimonial target.

Another slide change. More words rumbled from his throat. His voice was pure intellectual delight. She wrote faster. Really, she must start focusing on the images and not the man. But pressing concerns about the neurachnid's design rose to mind. Here was opportunity. What questions might she put to the great neurophysiologist before her? What flash of brilliant design might she reveal? What was the best path toward winning his regard?

Suddenly, the opportunity was upon her.

The screen went dark, and the room brightened. "If there are no questions," Lord Thornton began. "Tomorrow I will discuss..."

He would send them on their way with no opportunity to engage? She added arrogance to the list of his defining traits. "Professor, with regard to the ganglion, would you consider it possible to transform neurility into electricity via a rare earth metal?"

As intense, blue eyes turned to stare at her, Amanda fancied she'd caught the slightest slackening of his firm, square jaw before it tightened so much his lips thinned. She waited for his answer in breathless anticipation.

"My dear Miss...?" His eyebrows rose in both question and challenge.

"Ravensdale," she supplied. Something in his eyes crystallized, not into ice, but into something much harder and denser, something with razor sharp edges, and she met that piercing gaze with the uneasy sensation in her stomach that things were about to go badly awry.

"Miss Ravensdale. From your...fantastical question, I can only conclude that you have spent far too much time reading texts beyond your comprehension without adequate guidance. Despite their high electrical conductivity, insertion of such elements into the human body would be ethically reprehensible."

Amanda inhaled sharply at the implied reprimand. There were several smothered snickers behind her. Her eyes narrowed as they caught Lord Thornton's gaze. No. She was right and he knew it. With great deliberation, he'd chosen to belittle her hypothesis before her classmates. All hope of a demonstration of her neurachnid followed by his assistance evaporated like a drop of water falling on a hot coal. She pursed her lips, and his eyes flashed with victory.

The arrogant bastard.

Beside her, Simon drew an indignant breath. Amanda pressed her gloved palm to his arm, stifling his impulse to rush to her defense.

Then without further acknowledgement of his audience, Lord Thornton strode from the room.

Made in the USA
Middletown, DE
01 August 2017